BEYOND BEOWULF

BEYOND BEOWULF

❁

For Alex

Christopher L. Webber

Christopher L. Webber

iUniverse, Inc.
New York Lincoln Shanghai

Beyond Beowulf

iUniverse books may be ordered through booksellers or by contacting:

iUniverse
2021 Pine Lake Road, Suite 100
Lincoln, NE 68512
www.iuniverse.com
1-800-Authors (1-800-288-4677)

ISBN-13: 978-0-595-37358-1 (pbk)
ISBN-13: 978-0-595-67489-3 (cloth)
ISBN-13: 978-0-595-81755-9 (ebk)
ISBN-10: 0-595-37358-5 (pbk)
ISBN-10: 0-595-67489-5 (cloth)
ISBN-10: 0-595-81755-6 (ebk)

Printed in the United States of America

INTRODUCTION

The Story

Beowulf is one of those classic texts that help us understand the human condition. Set in a time as remote from ours as we can imagine, it shows us men and women who have attempted to impose an order, a civilization, on their lives, yet have found it disrupted again and again, as all human beings do, by forces of chaos both external to themselves and internal. The unknown poet who composed this saga at least 1,200 years ago, did, however, impose his own order on those chaotic events, as well as on the language with which he tells his story.

The strange thing is that, although the poem contains instances of foreshadowing throughout and ends with forebodings of disaster, no one in all the centuries since has written a sequel. *Beyond Beowulf* is an attempt to fill that gap. This poem is to *Beowulf* as the *Odyssey*, we might say, is to the *Iliad*: it is the journey that takes place when the battle is over. This sequel is filled with references to *Beowulf* itself but takes its general direction from historical evidence of migration from Scandinavia to the British Isles.

For those who are not familiar with the *Beowulf* saga, it can be briefly summarized as follows: A Danish king named Hrothgar has won fame and fortune and creates a great feasting hall to celebrate his achievements. No sooner do his warriors begin to feast, however, than a hulking monster called Grendel decides to destroy their happiness. When the warriors have feasted and have fallen into a drunken slumber, Grendel comes, snatches up and devours some warriors, and returns to his lair. For many years, these raids continue and Hrothgar's life is filled with sadness. Across the seas in Sweden, a young warrior named Beowulf hears of the situation and decides to remedy it. With a few companions, Beowulf crosses the sea and presents himself at Hrothgar's court. A feast is held, Beowulf tells something of his past achievements, and they all fall asleep. As usual, Grendel stops by for an evening meal but Beowulf grabs his arm and after a brief but horrific wrestling match, Beowulf tears off Grendel's arm. Grendel slinks home to die while the warriors nail his arm up to the gables and celebrate. Grendel's mother, however, soon arrives, seeking revenge, and she drags some warriors off to her lair for a meal. The next day, Beowulf and a few others follow her tracks and find a dark lake. Beowulf dives in, swims down, and finds an underwater cavern where Grendel lies mortally wounded. Beowulf fights Grendel's mother and kills her also. That evening there is more feasting, and Hrothgar delivers a sermon on the shortness and uncertainty of human life. Beowulf then returns to Sweden where, eventually, he becomes king of the Geats and reigns peacefully for many years. One day, however, a man happens upon a dragon's lair and unwisely removes a golden cup while the dragon sleeps. When the dragon wakens and discovers a cup is missing, he flies into the night sky breathing fiery death and destruction on the hapless citizens. Beowulf decides to deal with the dragon and, after an epic struggle in which he is mortally wounded, he kills the dragon with the help of a young relative named Wiglaf. Amid prophecies of doom, Beowulf's body is burned on a funeral pyre and a memorial mound is built on a headland so that sailors will see and remember.

Beyond Beowulf begins at this point. There are notes in the closing pages that point to many of the connections between *Beowulf* and this sequel.

In constructing this narrative, I have referred as often as possible to *Beowulf* itself but have relied, as well, on standard commentaries and histories. I have turned also to studies of the burials found in England at Sutton Hoo for information about the period and, especially, about the burials that took place there. It does seem that these burials were made by people who had much in common with the people of the *Beowulf* narrative and that Beowulf's people may, indeed, have come to East Anglia at about this time. So the narrative I have constructed may be fiction, but the critical events are historically possible and, in broad terms, even probable.

The Poetry

The poetry of Anglo-Saxon England was written (as most of today's poetry is not) for the ear, to be read aloud or, probably, sung with instrumental accompaniment. Most of the various translations that have been made try to catch the meaning more than the music. Or, if they do try to make the poetry sing, still very few do it while giving adequate emphasis to the quality that made it sing in its own day, and that is alliteration. We are familiar with poetry that rhymes and poetry that has a rhythmic stress pattern, but alliterative poetry is seldom today a basic feature of our poetry. But why not? Alliteration is still important to us, perhaps more important than we realize. We use it often for emphasis: we promise "to have and to hold," we speak of "time and tide," we "aid and abet" or "rant and rave." Alliteration still adds force to our speech. A sequel to *Beowulf* would hardly be recognizable as such if it failed to make some use of alliteration.

Specifically, *Beowulf* is composed of lines with four stresses of which two must begin with the same consonant or a vowel. The line is divided into two segments, often indicated by an asterisk or similar mark. The first stress of the second half-line is the key syllable, and at least one other syllable (but not the last stress) must alliterate with it.

Ideally, a sequel to *Beowulf* would use the same pattern. That I have not done so is a result of my feeling that, however well that pattern may have fit Old English, it fits much less well with the modern form of the language. Old English and Modern English, though they have many words and constructions in common, are very different languages. Critics speak of *Beowulf* as the first great poem in any modern European language, but no modern English speaker can read *Beowulf* in the original without a great deal of help. Perhaps most significant for anyone attempting to write a sequel to *Beowulf* is that the Anglo-Saxon of *Beowulf* is a polysyllabic language, while modern English is much more monosyllabic. The "four-letter Anglo-Saxon words" that we refer to so often were not characteristic of the *Beowulf* poet's Anglo-Saxon. He uses only five four-letter words in the first ten lines, while one standard translation (Howell D. Chickering, Jr.) uses thirteen. The *Beowulf* poet, employing a language filled with polysyllabic words (and adding to the problem by using and inventing compound words in almost every line), uses far fewer words per line.[1] At least 60 percent of the lines in *Beowulf* have five words or fewer, while almost 80 percent of the lines in Chickering's translation have seven words or more. No one can capture the meaning and poetry of *Beowulf* in modern English without using more words and, almost inevitably, a longer, looser line. The *Beowulf* poet could let alliteration dominate the sound pattern with two or three alliterated words or stressed syllables per line. In a modern translation that settles for two or three alliterated stresses in a longer line, the alliteration will play a much less dominant role.

It is worthwhile to note that alliteration was still a dominant pattern in fourteenth-century English poetry but that the Norman conquest had already introduced new patterns with a metered line and rhymed couplets. Gradually, this pattern made its influence felt. William Langland's great epic of that century, *Piers Plowman*, retains the alliterated form but uses a longer line with at least three alliterated stressed syllables per line: "On a May morning on a Malvern hillside…Chastity without charity shall be chained in hell…What is readiest to ripen rots soonest." But Langland is part of a last flowering of the alliterative style. Chaucer, in the same century, uses meter and rhyme and is deeply indebted to the French tradition. Middle English was, of course, more similar to modern English: words were shorter, and Langland and Chaucer alike necessarily use a longer line.

In constructing a sequel to *Beowulf*, therefore, I have not only followed the example of Langland in using at least three alliterated stresses per line but also attempted to give the alliteration increased prominence by fitting it within the classic English iambic pentameter, so that stress patterns are clear and stressed syllables prominent. Clearly this is not the pattern of the *Beowulf* poet, but it is, I believe, a pattern that preserves the feel of the original while, at the same time, providing a format that fits modern English comfortably.

Further Notes about Alliteration

Experts agree that *Beowulf* is written in lines with four stresses and that the third stress (first stress of the second half of the line) is the key. One stressed syllable in the first half-line must alliterate with that key stress; the second stressed syllable in the first half-line may also alliterate, but the second stressed syllable in the second half-line must not.[2] In *Beowulf*, the stressed syllable is almost always the first syllable of a word since that is where the stress normally falls in Old English. In modern English, on the other hand, the accented syllable of a word is often the second syllable or even the third. It is noticeable that modern translations of Beowulf often alliterate on the first letter of a word even though it is not the accented syllable. In effect, they are writing for the eye, while the Beowulf poet was writing for the ear. *Beyond Beowulf* alliterates on stressed syllables whether they are the first, second, or third syllable of a word. The eye may not see this as easily, but the alliteration will become clear when the line is read aloud.

The alliteration, it should be noted, treats all vowels as the same so that "It is my own first effort as an usher" would be considered an example of alliteration. The *Beowulf* poet also treats words beginning "sw" as different from words beginning with "s" alone. I have not continued this distinction, and I have tried to alliterate sounds rather than letters, so "know" and "nine" alliterate and "one" and "wonder"; "wolf," on the other hand, does not alliterate with "where," nor "ten" with "then," but "who" alliterates with "how." For the same reason, I have not used "one" as an alliterated vowel, but I have felt free to alliterate "s" words whether they are "sw" or "sh."

The reader should notice that what seems to the eye to be alliteration is not always so. "Ceaseless cares" is not an alliteration, but "ceaseless sounds" is. Seamus Heaney's new translation of *Beowulf* sometimes employs visual alliteration, but the *Beowulf* poet, composing primarily for auditors, would not have done so. *Beyond Beowulf* does not use visual alliteration, so it will be necessary to read some lines aloud to hear the alliteration that the eye may not notice.

I should also note that I have not attempted to set the alliteration around the third stressed syllable of the line. I have chosen not to use so strict a pattern that the alliteration would become too regular and dominating. I have been satisfied if three stressed words (or syllables) alliterate wherever they fall in the line.

1. Line 799 uses only two words, "hearðhicgende hildemecgas," and four-word lines are common.

2. Cf. Alexander, Michael, *Beowulf*, pp. xxv–bbxxvi, and *Beowulf: A Verse Translation*, pp. 47–48 and Chickering, Howell D., Jr., *Beowulf: A Dual Language Edition*, p. 33.

Beyond Beowulf

Attend! You sometimes still can hear the sound
Of flames in fury as the funeral pyre
Of Beowulf went blazing up; the bonfire
That caused the corpse to burn had carried with it
The heartfelt hopes of all the hero's folk
Who looked to him to lead them. They had lost
The one who went before them, waged their wars,
Who gave them gold, and helped them guard their homes.
The steadfast warriors stood about and stared
10   As if to find their future in the flames,
And lingered till at last the evening light
Had faded fully from the flaming sky,
Then drifted home to heal their aching hearts
With sleep, the silent cure of ceaseless cares.
Thick darkness then came down around their dwellings;
Around them roamed the beasts unruled by law
Who forage freely in the night for food
And catch and kill the creatures that they seek.

When morning came once more to Middle Earth,
20   The red sun rose and roused them from their rest,
God's candle cast its light across the world

On fertile fields and forests far away,
And sleepers stirred and slowly sought their friends.
A sense of dread and doom now weighed them down,
Of absence everywhere that all could feel,
The lack of that strong leader they had lost.
With slow and solemn steps they set to work;
They raked the ruined remnants of their houses
To search for something that was not consumed
30   By fire before the serpent's blazing fury,
The damage that the dragon's wrath had done.
They brought stout oaken beams to build anew
The high feast hall and people's simple homes.
At last the largest house was laid in order,
A handsome hall, though less than Heorot,
Well-braced with boards and bound with hammered iron,
A mead-hall meant for mighty warriors
To celebrate success in war, where bards could sing
And harpers help them raise the warriors' hearts
40   With tales of triumphs in the time gone by.
When darkness deepened at the end of day
The warriors walked into the wooden hall;
They filled their flagons, foaming ale was passed
From hand to hand around the feasting house.
One question came to all: Who will be king
Since now our guide and guardian is gone?
Some wondered whether Wiglaf was the one
Who might do most to make their foes afraid.
Undaunted by the dragon, Wiglaf dared
50   To battle in the burning flames with Beowulf
And wield the weapon left by Weohstan;

He struck his sword deep in the sky-Lord's throat.
But others, anxious for an older king,
A conqueror who had killed his foes in combat,
Were looking for a leader rather like
The kings that other countries counted on
To wage their wars and bring them rich rewards.

Then Sigelac, the strongest champion, stood,
A warrior battle-worn through many winters,
60   And called for quiet in the clamorous hall.
He struck his shield until the tumult ceased.
"The grief we share is great," so he began,
"And all of us are overcome with sorrow;
The leader that we loved, who shared our lives,
Who came to grips with Grendel long ago,
That marvelous man, who made the monster yield,
Was called by Glory's King to come with him
And find the far-off land for men of fame
That no one who is now among us knows.
70   He sleeps in silence, free of all life's struggles,
And honored even in his death by all of us;
His strength has brought us what we still possess:
The gifts of gold which he so freely gave.
We offer Wiglaf also every honor,
Though young in years, he would not yield to any
But battled bravely, there with Beowulf,
And someday, surely, he will strongly lead;
He fears no foe and will win lasting fame;
But meanwhile we must make our plans, take measures,
80   For truly these are times that threaten tempests;
Dark clouds are coming and we must be careful

As foes in fury come to fall upon us.
They will have heard our hero cannot hinder
Their taking all the treasure that we toiled for.
So let us look then for an able leader
Of strength and stature who can face such storms,
One who can give to us the gifts he garnered,
And such as I have stored away myself:
Bright rings of reddish gold and goblets wrought
90   By seasoned craftsmen using subtle skills,
Sharp biting battle-axes and well-burnished shields,
And cups deep cut in curious designs
By elvish artisans in ancient times.
Then come, my comrades, let me counsel you,
For everywhere our enemies are arming
And well aware of all our weaknesses.
Today we dare not dally; we must act."
The warriors struck their spears against their shields
Until the rafters rang; they cheered and roared
100   And shouted, "Sigelac!" A single mind
Now held those in the hall. The warriors hoped
To act, and so to ease their anxious minds.
They saw in Sigelac a man to suit their mood.
The oldest warrior, Aelric, watched them all
But did not stand or shout. It seemed to him
That he could smell the smoke of smoldering fires
And see the black flames and the buildings burning
And hear the howl of wolves and women wailing,
Lamenting men returning nevermore,
110   But no one noticed that he never moved.
Then cups of mead were carried round; the crowd

Rejoiced and joined their friends in joyous song
Until at last they let the lights go out,
The flaming torches flickered as they failed.
Then men made beds with bolsters on the wooden boards,
And weary soldiers sank down to their sleep.

When birdsong broke out and the daylight broadened
They sent a summons to the sleep-drenched men
From Sigelac to stand with him and swear
120   Allegiance to their leader, to be loyal
To him their chosen chief and champion.
They gathered round him on the growing grass,
And came together clothed as if for combat;
The earls were all well-armed with ash wood spears,
And proud to go campaigning with companions
Whose mettle had been measured many times.
When Sigelac had seen them all he spoke,
A veteran whose voice was vehement,
The son of Selibrod, a seasoned fighter:
130   "I summoned you to stand with me and strike
Our foes with fear as fighters ought to do,
All those abroad held back by Beowulf
Through soft and kindly seasons. On all sides
Our neighbors knew that they could not attack
Our homes while he, our champion, was here,
But we have gained no gold and won no glory;
Our youths who yearn to fight as young men should
Have never drawn a sword or dealt the death blow
Or seen the steaming blood that spurts from wounds.
140   We lie here far too long like wolves in lairs
Who keep their cubs with care but never go

To forage for their food and fail to teach
Their offspring any of the arts of war.
But peace has poisoned us. Let us prepare
Our swords for slaughter and to slay our foes,
So we shall garner glory for the Geats
And take home treasure to enrich our tribe;
The world shall wonder at the fame we win
And all the trophies that we take in triumph."
150   Then Wiglaf said, "The world may wonder also
What failings of our foes offended us
Enough to cause such killing and such carnage.
The Geats are loyal to leaders; let them hear.
Then we will follow faithfully as friends
And comrades in a common course of action."
The men around him murmured; many thought
It wrong to raise such questions. In a rage
They shook their spears and shouted, "Sigelac!"
A few, who had not fought before, were fearful,
160   While others, undecided, asked each other
To give them guidance: whether they should go
To far and distant fields in search of fame
Or stay and seek for safety in their homes.
Their eyes turned then to Aelric, oldest of them,
Both gray and gaunt with years, and greatly honored,
One who, at every turn, would tell the truth.
His voice was low; they leaned toward him to listen.
Then Aelric said in slow and solemn tones,
"I wish I had the wisdom I had once
170   As to the future which the fates have fashioned.
The years have passed, and yet I once was young

And eager to acquire the archers' art.
My sight was sharp then and my hands were steady;
When I had sent my arrow on its way
The shaft could split a distant slender reed,
But then a breeze, a breath, could bend the reed
And override my arrow's careful aim
And so the shot I took could go astray
However good the guidance that I gave.
180   I sought to get myself a sailor's skills
And ventured very far on voyages
Across the cold, black seas to foreign coasts
Where grapes are grown and where the grass is green
In March, and I saw many other marvels,
And I have learned some lessons in my life:
I have been taught you cannot turn the tides
Or steer a ship against a storm-tossed sea.
I learned the human heart can hold much evil
And also good, but what the gods will give us,
190   I think that none can know. How can we name
A force we cannot fathom? We are feathers,
And we are blown about by every breeze."
The ranks were growing restless, ripe for action;
They did not like to listen very long.
The son of Selibrod then called for silence.
"Too many words," he said, "can muddy minds;
Since Wiglaf asked a question, I will answer.
I might remind you of the messenger
Who brought you baleful news of Beowulf
200   And told you tales of terror soon to come.
He said the Swedes would sweep us all away,

The Scylfing spearmen, striving for revenge,
Who think their threats will throw us into flight.
But they have killed our kings; when Hathcyn came
To land they lurked in hiding, launched their spears,
And Ongentheow rushed from unseen ambush
And struck his helmet so he sank and died.
Onela also, honest as he was,
Struck Herdred, son of Hygelac; he hit
210   And broke his bone-cage with a broad axe stroke.
And after that his brother's offspring also
Was slain as slaughter spread and valiant men,
Though brave and true, were beaten down in blood.
Why should we wait and let them work their will?
Let us now venture victory and revenge;
Let those who will keep watch with Wiglaf here
Until the time when we return in triumph.
I call on you to come with me and conquer."

The warriors then went willingly to work
220   To bring aboard the ring-prowed dragon boats
The gleaming armor they had gladly gathered:
The hardened helmets and the chain mail hauberks,
The spears and swords and sturdy linden shields.
Above the boat they hoisted colored banners
That shone and glistened in the setting sun.
The heroes then came to the high-roofed hall,
The seasoned fighters sought to celebrate
Their comradeship and courage in the conflict
That they faced. They found their places; food was brought.
230   The mead bowls passed among them; merriment
Increased as warriors cast their cares away.

A bard sang ballads of the bravery
Of heroes such as Hygelac, whose horn
Had signaled slaughter of the Swedes
At Ravenswood; their ruler's reign was ended.
He struck his hand upon the harp he held,
His clear voice carrying across the hall,
And sang of Beowulf, who boldly battled
The monster, Grendel's mother, in the mere
240 And dealt a death blow to the fiery dragon
Whose wrath had rained down ruin on them all.
He also told a tale of distant travel,
When Beowulf had brought them strange-shaped bones
Of serpents of a size no one had seen.
He went with other warriors toward the west,
For some had said that there were sun-warmed lands
Where golden stones lie gleaming on the ground,
Where snow and ice are very seldom seen,
And bubbling springs restore the sightless eyes
250 And withered limbs, and wanderers are welcomed
By maids with mead so sweet and marvelous
That all are overcome with ecstasy,
And none who tread that soil return to tell
The way. Their chief had chosen champions
And well-made, wide-bowed, wooden ring-necked ships.
They stocked them well with spears and shields
And all the weapons warriors would want
And shoved the sturdy ships away from shore,
The carved prows cutting through the cold, gray waves
260 And taking them in time to towering cliffs
Where thick, green glaciers thawed and thundered down

And made great mountains, melting as they floated
Upon the sea, a sight unseen before
By any of the Geats, who watched in awe.
They stared at seals and certain white-winged birds
That skim the waves. Still working further west
They found at last a lifeless, barren land,
A wild and windswept, wintry kind of place.
They did not stay but steered still further south
270   Until the weather was more mild and warm,
And there they found a fine and fertile land
Where grapes were growing, green on ancient vines.
The natives fled away at first in fear;
They had not seen such helmets, hiding faces,
And burnished bright with gold, prepared for battle,
High-crowned and crafted with great care and skill,
Embellished with the heads of boars and bears,
That gave the Geats a grim and fearful look
That filled the native folk at first with fear.
280   But then they got a glimpse of golden rings
And saw the wrought iron spear-tips and the swords
And came back creeping very cautiously
To offer beads and broken stones in barter
And certain fruits and finely finished furs,
But Beowulf forbade the men to bargain
Lest one of them be wounded by their weapons.
But when ignored, the natives made a dreadful noise
And set upon the soldiers suddenly,
Who, caught off guard, could barely beat them back,
290   Although they slaughtered some of them with swords.
Then others in the woods let fly their arrows

And wounded Wulfric and two other warriors.
Without their battle bows, the Geats drew back
And sent their ships back out to sea.
They went no further west but wondered still
How far the ocean flows. They did not find
A land of light and sun. But when at last
They set their sails toward home a monstrous serpent
With dreadful fangs and eyes that flashed like fire
300   Bore down on them with dreadful speed and drove
Its head against their hollow boat. In horror
They saw it wrap itself in rings around
The boat with Beowulf on board. It crushed
The oaken beams with ease and all seemed lost.
It gripped one Geat within its gruesome jaws
And diving downward dragged him to the depths
To make his meal. The two remaining boats
Then pulled companions from the pounding waves
And set their sails to flee away in sorrow.
310   But Beowulf forbade them, kept the boats
On watch and waiting in the swirling waves,
Imagining the monster might return
To search for sailors for a second meal.
With twine they tied the ships together tightly
To keep the serpent's coils from crushing them
And circled slowly in the sullen waves,
They drifted, filled with dread, in dwindling circles,
And wondered whether one of them might well
Be next to know the monster's teeth and nails.
320   Then, suddenly, the serpent struck their boats
From underneath, and all at once came up

With Ferlag's blood still flowing from its fangs
And battered hard against the boats' stout boards
Till Beowulf could dive and dig his dagger
Into the serpent's scales with all his strength.
The creature coiled around him, carried him
Back down in darkness to its dwelling place.
A coal-black cavern crammed with dead men's bones.
The hero drove his dagger deeper still
330   And hung on tight behind the monster's head
So that it could not catch him in its claws.
It tried; it turned and twisted terribly
And hoped to hold the hero in its claws
Or take him in its terrifying teeth
And break his bone-cage. Beowulf held on,
And, slowly sliding forward, stuck his dagger
In brain, beneath the bone, above the neck.
It did not die but made a desperate lunge
And, hissing horribly, it heaved its back
340   Against a granite wall to grind the champion
To death; but, dropping down to draw his sword,
He quickly struck to cut the creature's head off.
He sliced through bone and sinew with his sword.
Although his blade was broken by the bone,
He cut the coiling carcass into pieces.
Meanwhile above, his brothers in the boat
Saw boiling blood and bits of mangled flesh
Come surging up to stain the swollen waves,
But looked in vain and feared their leader lost
350   Until, quite suddenly, they saw him swimming
Toward them holding up the horrid head.

They tied it to the side; they would not take
The scabrous thing inside the ship with them.
Then, hoisting sails, they headed for their homes;
They steered their sea-steed through the stiffening breeze
And windblown waves. The weeks away at sea
Had left them longing for the homes they loved.

The champions cheered the song the singer chanted.
The bard sang on of battles, brave deeds done,
360   Of foes defeated, friendships formed, and how
The gods had molded Middle Earth for mortals
With forests, fields, and oceans stretching far.
His clear voice called the names of conquerors
Whose grief and glory are forgotten now.
He sang of love and loss; he sang of loyalty.
They filled the flagons up with foaming ale
And warriors laughed and lingered still to listen
To tales of tribal triumph and defeat.

When morning came, they met and made their way
370   Toward the boats; the brave men climbed aboard.
The salty spray was splashing over them
As eager men pushed off the beach and out
To deeper water in the waves and wind
While Sigelac himself hauled up the sails
Of wave-birds taking warriors on their way.
The ships grew smaller as they sailed away
And, dim and distant, finally disappeared
As Wiglaf watched them from the water's edge.

For days the weather darkened, clouds came down,
380   And black-clad ravens brooded in the branches.

The howl of wolves was heard at noon; on high
An eagle circled in the sullen sky.
But meanwhile, with so many men away,
The women went about their daily work
While chimneys smoked and children chased each other—
A time of peace. The people worked and played,
But sometimes brooded, too, about the battle
And wondered if the warriors were well.
At last a lone survivor, limping, bloodstained,
390   His clothes in tatters, torn by briars and trees,
And worn and weary after weeks of traveling
Appeared, his gaunt and pain-filled face gave proof
Of sorrow and of suffering he had seen.
He almost fell before they fetched a bench
And made him sit. He sank upon it sighing,
"They all are lost, and I alone am left;
They struck us down and Sigelac is slain."
Some women went to him and washed his wounds
While others found some food to set before him,
400   And as he ate, in eagerness to ask,
They pressed upon him, pleading to be told
About the battle, but he could not speak
So tired was he from travel and from terror.
His name was Wolferth, one of those who went
To fight the Frisians in a deadly feud
When Daeghrefne had died, a dauntless hero,
And Beowulf had brought back battle armor,
By strength and skill across the heaving sea.
At last they led him in and let him rest

410   On bolsters in the banquet hall; they bade him
        To sleep awhile and so regain his strength.

        The sun had set before they sought him out
        And woke him, wanting any further word,
        So he began again to speak and groaned,
        "All lost, all dead, and I alone am left;
        The sword consumed strong Sigelac and all
        Are gone, our gallant Geats, a grievous day.
        They set upon us suddenly. The Swedes
        Will come and kill us all; we cannot hope
420   That we can stand against their savage strength.
        A massacre, too many more than we,
        Too few, too foolish, food for wolves and ravens."
        But Wiglaf struck him; "Stop and start again,"
        He said, "And try to tell us, if you can, the truth:
        What happened? Who is dead? And how have you
        Escaped? We need to know your news at once.
        So tell us all you know of it in order:
        You set out on the ship and sailed away;
        We have not seen you since, so you must speak,
430   And tell us all until your safe return.
        Speak slowly so we can be sure to hear."
        He took a breath and, trembling, told his tale.
        He said, "You saw us as we sailed away
        In careless confidence that we would conquer,
        With shining armor stowed aboard our ship,
        God's beacon shining brightly on our banners,
        And all of us so eager for the fight;
        So we enjoyed our journey, and we joked
        About the beating we would bring the Swedes.

440 Our course was close to shore; we did not keep
A watch, or worry. There were often woods
Beside the shore, but once I thought I saw
A horseman high upon an open hill;
I think that they had placed a coastguard there
Who signaled somehow that our ships were coming.
But we were willing to go on our way
Without a thought of any lurking evil.
How could we be so confident and careless?"

His sobs were surging up, and so he stopped
450 To calm himself; he could not keep on talking
Until some time had passed. He took deep breaths
And slowly then went on. "I think that they
Were waiting for us, and so we, unwary,
Were trapped and caught. Their finest troops attacked us
From hiding, hit us; it was horrible.
Our soldiers, suddenly, were falling slain."

Then Wiglaf asked, "But was there no one wise
Enough to know, did none of you remember
How Ongentheow acted once to end
460 The life of Hathcyn, Hrethel's son, or how
He lured them to his trap; he let them land
And waited in the woods till like a wolf
He sprang upon our scattered reckless soldiers
And cut our king down with his cruel blade.
He slaughtered many with the slashing sword
While others fell with arrows in their flesh;
He soaked the Swedish soil with blood of Geats
And left the bloody bodies all unburied

For carrion crows to come and eat their fill.
470 There was no place to walk not wet with blood.
You can be sure the Scylfings still recall
That Weohstan, my father, was the warrior
Whose sharpened edge killed Eanmund in exile.
His brother, Eadgils, broods still on that blow
And holds the hope forever in his heart
To meet with me at last and make me pay
For what my father did—a futile feud
That only answers death with death unending.
But let us hear your story, how it happened
480 That all are lost and you are left alive."
They gathered close and he began again
But went on in a weak and wavering voice
So quietly they could not always catch
The sense of what he said, weighed down by sorrow:

"Yes, we had heard of Hathcyn's death, and how
The Swedes had set on him and slain them all,
But we imagined it a matter more
Of ballads sung by bards while drinking beer
Since those who did those deeds were now long dead;
490 We did not think that they could threaten us
With all our armor and our untried swords.
We brought our boats to shore and on the beach
We saw no sign of life. It seemed most strange
That every house was empty; all were gone.
The soldiers started looting, setting fires,
And taking back their trophies to the boats.
Then suddenly, assailed on every side,
The barbs came in above our battle shields,

The arrows flew at us and fighters fell.

500   Our ancient enemy it was, named Eadgils,

The Swedish sovereign now, who smote us first;

His fierce blade fell on us like fangs of wolves

And bit our bodies till the red blood flowed.

Our shields were shattered by his smashing blows;

The linden gave a little less protection.

We could not ward off well his dreadful war-strokes;

And then I saw him set on Sigelac

With all his force, as if to end his days.

They swung their swords, the clashing iron resounded

510   All through the woods as both men wielded weapons

Well forged of finest iron and flashing brightly

As helms and hauberks on both sides were hit.

Then Sigelac was stunned as Eadgils' sword

Had hit his head a blow beneath the helmet.

Blood spurted out, came streaming down his shoulders,

And blinded him with gore; a ghastly garment

He staggered, stunned, and slumped down to the ground,

Where Eadgils' dagger dealt a deadly blow.

He had no breath to boast of battle-deeds.

520   The doomed fell dead; the din of battle rose.

Then soldiers scattered everywhere and some

Less firm as fighters looked for ways to flee;

Their leader being lost, they longed for home,

But Eadgils followed fiercely, felling them

Along the way, in woods and wilderness.

The Scylfings' spears were thudding into shields;

Their proud spears pierced the soldiers' plaited armor.

I saw two Swedes attack the son of Modril,

The mighty Malric in a savage mood;
530   He cut down one of them, whose corpse grew cold.
The other Scylfing, aiming to do evil,
Then threw his spear at Malric's shield, which shattered;
But Malric meted out a mortal wound,
Sliced through his throat, a deadly, fatal thrust.
But several Scylfings then beset him roundly
And beat him down with many bitter blows
Until he toppled on the tawny earth.
I could not make out more amid the strife,
The clash and clangor of the raging conflict;
540   I sought to help but was assailed myself
By other Scylfings, all of them well armed.
I set upon a Scylfing, swung my sword,
And hit his helmet; he remained unhurt
And turned on me, a tall man, twice my size,
And raised his sword. I stabbed him in the stomach;
He groaned and hit the ground. I glanced around
But someone struck me from behind. I saw no more.
The next I knew, it was already night;
I lay there, looking for some light to see,
550   And heard the sound of Scylfings celebrating,
And far away a blazing fire. I feared
The worst, but wanting to be sure, I went,
Most carefully; I crept so close I heard
Them boast that birds would eat the Geatish bodies,
And so I heard them speak of Sigelac,
Of Modric, Byrhtwulf, and of many more
Whom they had slaughtered with their Swedish swords.
I dared not linger, listening to them laugh,

For fear at morning light the foe would find me.

560   I tried to run, but I was tripped and torn
By briars and branches till my hands were bleeding.
At last I lay down, longing for the day.
The night was full of noises; nameless forms
Were gliding past, perhaps of ghost or ghouls
Or shades of soldiers all too lately slain
And haunting me or hunting for a home,
A realm to rest in while their bodies rotted.
They had not heard of heaven's promised peace.
I clutched my sword and kept it close at hand

570   And bent my back against the biggest tree
But failed to free myself of horrid fears
Of green-eyed wolves that gathered in the gloom
And specters worse than that that set me shuddering.

"When morning came, I meant to make my way
Toward the south when sun's light showed me how,
But clouds had covered it; I could not see
And wandered woefully in trackless woods
Until I heard, behind me, high above,
The screams of eagles circling as they sought

580   For carrion corpses on the killing fields.
And so I went away through wilderness
Until I came to cliffs along the coast
And followed them, although afraid of falling
Where cracks and crevices lay covered up
By tangled roots of trees; there was no trail.
One day I did fall down and hurt myself;
I stopped the bleeding, bound it with a bandage,
And so I limped the last few leagues to home."

His feeble voice then flamed up in his fury:
590　"But now we must assemble spears and shields
And all the other implements of war
And arm ourselves against the Scylfing scourge
And vow to gain revenge and victory."

But Wiglaf said, "I think that we should wait
And think before we start to threaten them;
So many wives are widows, warriors dead.
We all are in an agony of grief
And troubled by your tale. We need some time
To ponder and to plan. I would propose
600　We meet again tomorrow; meanwhile all
Must study what you said. What shall we do:
Submit or find a way to fight or flee?"

When dawn came up next day, Wiglaf had drawn
A circle in the sand; he said to them,
"The lands are very large and we are little;
The Scylfings surely know our circumstance
And will be well aware that we are helpless
Before their fury. When their feasting ends
Their ships will sail and they will seek us out
610　And who will help us then? Where will we hide?
Our fighting men have fallen; we are few.
Our brothers, bold and fearless, have been beaten;
Their doom was death. Is that our destiny?"
But many of the men were murmuring
And Lofric said, "We cannot leave this land.
Our fathers were not frightened by their foes;
Our hearts and hearths and heritage are here,

So let us meet our doom and dare to die
As we defend our fields and families,
620   And win the warrior's wealth: a lasting fame."
Then champions cheered and chain mail hauberks rang,
But Herbrund said, "No fame can feed the famished
Nor does it make good milk in mothers' breasts
When babes are bawling and the cupboard bare.
If we cannot defend these fields, we ought to find
A place where we can pass our days in peace.
What glory do we gain by bearing grudges,
The ceaseless strife of Geatish folk with Swedes?
Why is it not as noble to ignore
630   The endless insults of an enemy
And follow peace to find a fuller life?
The dragon built its bed within the barrow
To rest on riches rusting in the ground,
As useless now as ever it has been.
What good is gold when we are in our graves?
I am a farmer first; my family
Is more to me than any mound of treasure.
When springtime comes and sunshine warms the soil
And soft rain washes winter snows away,
640   The sun unlocks the lakes, turns loose the streams
To flow down into rivers filled with fish,
And berries form on every bramble bush,
And children prate and play behind the plow,
I set out then to sow the bursting seed,
Inhale the odor earth is breathing out.
What more could any mortal man require?
Is that not all that anyone can ask?

But where the dead now dwell, they do not farm;
In hell they do not hold or hug their children,
650   Or swim in streams or stretch out in the sun.
If we are weak and cannot well stay here,
Then let us look for other lands to farm.
I love this land, but I will let it go
For peace and pay whatever price we must
To give that gift to those whose lives we guard."
Again some men were murmuring and many
Began to shout that they would smite the Scylfings
And find great fame and finally win glory.
Then gray-haired Aelric, gaunt and grizzled, spoke:
660   "Where were these fighters, now so fond of fame,
When Beowulf was battling in the blaze
And suffering the swirling surge of fire;
He was our king, but comrades did not come
To stand beside him when the dragon struck
Or brave the battle, bolting to the woods
To save their lives. But now they strut their strength
And urge us all to emulate their conduct.
Such people earn our pity, not our praise.
I save my scorn for scoundrels such as these,
670   Who lack the loyalty they owe their leader,
Abandon him in battle. Beowulf
Would never need such noble earls as these.
But he is dead; indeed, he met his doom,
And now we need to find another leader.
The Swedes will soon be seeking for our blood
And Wiglaf is the one as we all know
Who long was loyal and who can lead us now."

But Wiglaf, son of Weohstan, the warrior,
While standing in the circle, said to them,
680   "I would not fight a war we cannot win;
I see that some of you still seek a feud.
I would not fight a war we cannot win,
But I would rather rule our lives with reason.
I cannot be what Beowulf has been,
Who went to war as one against our foes
And often, even so, went out unarmed.
I cannot lead unless we are allied;
A hero has his strength, but I must hope
To fight with friends and find a way together.
690   I heard what Herbrund had to say
And feel as he does that these fields and farms
Are beautiful and hold the buried bones
Of forebears, fathers, friends whom we hold dear.
And yet, in years gone by, as you must know
Those forebears came from far to find this land
And when they came across the white-flecked whale-road
They found no fertile fields, but wilderness,
Deep forest filled with every form of life
But harsh and hostile to the human race.
Our toil has turned the sullen turf to bread
700   And made these frozen northern fields be fruitful.
We labored long to win this land, and yet
It was not always ours; it does not own us."
He moved to put some points well set apart
Within the circle, saying, "Swedes are here,
The Franks are here, and Frisians flourish there;
The dauntless Danes undoubtedly are here,

Our homes are here, but how much more there is!
Outside the circle I have drawn, they say,
Are islands and, it may be, other lands;
710   Some say the world is warmer in the west.
I hope to find such havens for my home
And call on you to come and to discover
A place of peace and new prosperity."
Then Herbrund said, "I hope for happiness;
My family follows you to find this country
And look for life, not death, and lasting peace."
The others echoed him and offered Wiglaf
Their loyalty, though some were sullen still.
Then Wiglaf warned that they should keep a watch
720   On Hronesness, on Götland's highest headland,
Upon the barrow built for Beowulf,
And set a soldier there to send them word,
If any evidence of enemies were seen,
A man to signal if the Swedish ships
Should come in sight along the curving coast,
An adverse omen. Then they all went home
To work with wives, to find out what they wanted
And gather all the gear to go with them:
The cups and crude spoons from their cottages,
730   And bowls and broaches, bits of jewelry,
Small heirlooms, all the family owned and valued,
And flax and cloth and flagons filled with mead
And shanks of bacon, salted beef, and bread
As food to feed them as they traveled far;
All these they brought down to the bay, where boats
Were safely sheltered on the rocky shore.

Then daylight dimmed, the disc of heaven faded,

And nighttime came to cast its heavy curtain,

As black as wings of ravens, baleful birds,

740   Upon the fertile fields and foaming shore,

The men all made their way into the mead-hall

While women called the children, kept them quiet

With tales of terrors in the tomblike night,

And sang the babies songs to help them sleep

Though they were threatened by the thought of change,

An unknown future, and an alien soil.

The men had meanwhile gathered in the mead-hall

In hope of hearing what the future held,

What country could be found across the sea

750   And far away for weary wanderers,

Who hope for haven in a heartless world

And for a better future for themselves.

Then Wiglaf said, "The world is large, but we

Are not alone, our need unknown to friends.

The oldest of our soldiers often said

That Hrothgar had pledged help to Beowulf

And said the realm he ruled and all its riches

Should all be shared across the seabirds' bath

Whenever needs were known to one another,

760   And ringed-prowed ships, across the surging seas,

Should bring our people presents, proofs of love.

He said they would stand firm toward foe and friend,

And always aid us in our hour of need.

The time has come for us to test the truth

Of all that Hrothgar said and seek for safety

Among our friends the Danes. I do not doubt

That many will remember still the monster
Called Grendel, gruesome fiend who grieved them all
Through twelve long winters, working woeful harm
770   And having his own way at Heorot
Until the son of Ecgtheow saved the Scyldings
And broke the bones of Grendel. Beowulf
Befriended them and fought that fearful monster,
Tore off his arm and nailed it up as proof.
So now, when Geats have need of help, I know
The world is large but we will find a welcome
Among the Danes." The doubters did not protest,
But many murmured still among themselves
And waited. Then came Yrfa, Wiglaf's wife,
780   Raised high her golden cup and hailed the heroes;
She went to Wiglaf, then to everyone,
And poured the amber ale for each to quaff.
Then gaiety began to grow and spread
Within the hall as heroes hailed each other
And men dispelled their doubts by drinking deeply.
A bard sang ballads of a bygone day
When Geats had gone to war and garnered glory
Against the Swedes with dagger, sword, and spear.
But soon he sang as well of storied journeys
790   To unknown, ancient lands beyond the ocean
Where dreadful sights are seen and dragons dwell;
He sang of sailors, those whose spirits soar
In pain and peril on the plunging waves,
When they can ride the swell of storms at sea
And dawn is darkened with the driving snow,
The frost and falling sleet and freezing rain,

Who love the loneliness and long salt-surge,
The storm-drenched eagle's scream and sea mew's call,
That haunt the homebound sailor hopelessly.
800   He sang of wild and wailing winds and howling gale;
He sang of seas like mountains, surging tides,
And waves that washed a ship's whole crew away.
They struggled in the swirling sea and sank
To find the fish that feed on sailors' bones;
Their widows wailed and orphaned children wept.
At last he sang of loneliness and love,
The comfort of one's comrades and one's kin,
And friends in foreign lands, who never found
Their homelands anymore; their hearts were heavy.
810   He finished. Fighters slept upon the floor.

The sun was dim next day and clouds were dark.
The Geats were gathered on the shore in groups
Where Wiglaf went to them and warned them, saying,
"The hardest time is here; I had not told you
That we must set ablaze and burn our buildings,
The hearths and homes that we have held so dear,
Where babes were born and we have broken bread,
The houses we inherited, the hall
Where we have sung our joy and shared our sorrows.
820   We cannot leave the least of our belongings;
The Scylfings must not say that they destroyed it
Or be allowed to boast of beating us."
The fighters than pulled faggots from the fire
And turned to take the torches through the village
And there ignite each house's thick reed thatch.
The hungry flames spread fast and filled the air

With stinging smoke that drove the soldiers back.
The warriors meanwhile went about their work
Till ships were stocked and families safe on board,
830   The people in the boats. They pushed the prows
Away from shore where smoke and soot still rose
In grayish wisps against the gathering clouds
And left the land behind, not looking back.
The sea was quiet and the ships went smoothly
Across the water and the windswept waves.
Though lonely in the limitless expanse,
Unending aspect of the open sea,
They steered the ships toward the hidden sun,
A brightness breaking through the brooding clouds
840   And shining softly in the distant south.

The Scylfings saw the smoke while sailing south
And wondered what it was that would create
So dark a stain against the southern sky.
They brought their dragon boats into the bay
To find a fire-dark land. The flames had died
But smoldered still amid the smell of death
That rose around them from the ruined homes.
They stood and stared, amazed at what they saw;
The thought that came to all of them was this:
850   "The Franks or Frisians must have come here first
And gained a victory, so the Geats are gone."
They brushed aside the blackened thatch and beams
To look for any loot that might be left
But they found only ashes underneath;
No glory could be gained by gathering them.
Then some were saying they should seek their homes

Before the Franks or Frisians should go there
And make that unprotected place their prey.
The saddened Swedes returned then to their ships,
860   Their dreams of gold and battle glory gone,
And, disappointed, put their oars in place
And set their sails toward home—a sorry lot.
The Geats went on and soon began to glimpse
Through darkening clouds the distant Danish coast,
A low and purple line of solid land,
A welcome sight for wet and weary folk.
At last the ships came sliding to the shore
Where Beowulf had come to beach his boat
And help King Hrothgar who had long despaired
870   Of gaining peace. He stayed in Grendel's grip
So long as life stayed in that loathsome monster.
The coastguard keeping watch upon a cliff
On horseback hurried down to hail the Geats,
A mounted force of five, all fully armed,
Whose leader quickly called them to account:
"How dare you draw your prows to Danish soil?"
He asked; "I see that some of you are soldiers
And armed as I am, able to contend
With sentries such as we are, stationed here.
880   But I must tell you we have twenty times
As many men prepared to meet with you
Unless you leave our shore before much longer.
And yet I see that some of you are young
And you have women with you. If you want
To fight, I fear your families will suffer.
So now reply, and promptly, if you please,

Because you cannot otherwise come closer
Until you tell me what your titles are
And names and nation. I must know all this
890   For enemies are often on our shores
And we have suffered serious harm from some,
So we must warn our troops to treat you well
If you are friends, or fight if you are foes.
Who are you? I must have an answer now."
Then Wiglaf was the first to speak; "I will,"
He said, "reply; our purpose here is peaceful.
You should be glad to greet us; we are Geats.
We boast that Beowulf has been our king.
Your realm was rescued from the reign of terror
900   When his strong hand defeated Grendel here;
The monster and his mother met their match.
Then Hrothgar gave our leader golden gifts
And promised peace between our peoples always
And aid if either one had any need;
But now our nation also stands in need.
My name is Wiglaf and I wish for words
With him who holds the throne of Hrothgar now
To ask whatever aid it may seem right
To give in gratitude for Grendel's death."
910   The coastguard said, "It is our king who can
Command concerning this; his throne is over there
Beyond those trees. I will send two to take you
Into the hall where Hrethor has his throne.
Choose ten to take with you and tell the rest
To stay here on the shore till we receive
Our orders. I must always stay on guard

And watch the water and the other ways
That lead toward our land. Now you must leave
Your sword and spear right here beside the ships.
920   Our king requires that we take utmost care."
Then Wiglaf chose some wives to go as well
And bring their babies so they'd seem to be
More like a family than a force to fear.
Two men in helm and hauberk hastened then
To go as guides for them to greet the king.
They followed these men from the floating ships,
Now reined by ropes and riding in the bay.
The stony street led straight up from the shore;
They hoped to see the hall that Hrothgar built,
930   Its gables decked with gleaming gold, its glory
And splendor shone through sundry foreign lands,
But all they saw was empty space and ashes,
The blackened beams and empty, burned-out shell
Of Heorot, King Hrothgar's feasting hall.
A sorry sight. They stood and stared in horror.
Around the hall's debris were humble homes,
A few of farmers and their families;
The sentry showed them somewhat further on
A larger house. "This is King Hrethor's hall,"
940   He said, and summoned others from inside;
A tall retainer came and talked with them.
He said, "I serve King Hrethor, and it seems
That you are exiles, asking for our aid,
With many mouths to feed. Why, may I ask,
Should Hrethor help you? He is often asked
By poor and piteous people, persecuted,

And driven here half-dead, in dreadful shape,
And we would willingly deal kindly with them
If we were safe ourselves. But you have seen
950   Our royal residence, destroyed, in ruins.
The Frisian forces came with flame and sword
To gain some glory; they did us no good.
They slaughtered some of our best soldiers
Whose constant courage we had counted on,
Destroyed and sacked our winter stores as well.
We drove them off, but damage had been done
That weakened us." But Wiglaf, tired of waiting,
Broke in to ask, "May I point out to you
That we are Geats, and Hrothgar gladly gave
960   Assurance of assistance and his succor,
Affirmed a friendship forged against all rivals
And loyalty lasting through the length of years.
We came to see your king in confidence
That Hrothgar's heart-oath would be held in honor."
Then Wittu answered them, a wary watchman,
A sentry certain to maintain in safety,
His country's king, entrusted to his care:
"We often overlook the deeds of old
In troubled time like these, but I will tell
970   Our leader, Lord of Scyldings, you would like
To speak with him, and soon bring his response.
If you will wait, I will return at once."
He strode then swiftly to the seat of Hrethor
A leader young in years and yet respected
By friend and foe alike, a forthright king.
Acquainted with the customs of the court,

He waited willingly; then Wittu said:
"Some comrades came today, a Geatish cohort,
Whose boats have borne them well above the brine;
980   Their leader, Wiglaf, wishes words with you
And brings to mind our bond with Beowulf.
It seems to me that you should meet this man
Although I think the stores we have are thin."
King Hrethor said, "I have most surely heard
Of Wiglaf, son of Weohstan, a Waegmunding,
And last of all that line, a likely heir
To Beowulf, most loyal and brave in battle.
His dagger gave the death stroke to the dragon
Whose rage and fury filled the Danes with fear.
990   I very much would like to meet this man,
This prince, now present here. So, please, go back
And urge him to come in and speak with us."
Then Wittu went to Wiglaf once again
And said that Hrethor had invited him
To draw near and address the Danish monarch.
He said to him, "You may present yourself;
So come; our king is curious to hear
The story of your struggle and your sojourn.
His majesty remembers many tales
1000   Of Beowulf and begs that you will bring
Some good news of the glory of the Geats,
A war-strong people whom he wishes well;
He gladly reaffirms our former friendship."
Then Wiglaf went with him; they walked together,
The steadfast soldiers in their shining armor,
And with them went their wives and children also,

Both tired and tearful from their traveling.
King Hrethor said, the stalwart Danish sovereign,
"I wish to welcome you most warmly here.
1010   Our peoples promised one another peace
In former days; I would confirm that faith
And pray that both our peoples prosper always.
King Hrothgar held this throne by heaven's favor,
And made a mead-hall, mightiest of all,
A splendid, stately building, standing here,
But Grendel grieved him greatly with his raids,
A monster moved by hateful spite and malice
Who ruled the royal mead-hall ruthlessly
Until your uncle offered aid to us
1020   And freed us from the fierce grip of that spirit.
But Hrothgar died and Hrothulf, Halga's son,
Usurped the throne and slew King Hrothgar's son.
Then Heoreweard killed him and held the throne
Until his death. The Danes endured all this
But, weakened woefully, were warred against
By Frisians, then by Franks; the fierce Hetware
And other enemies assaulted us.
We fought the Franks but failed to drive them off
Till torch-fire turned the tragic hall to ashes,
1030   A day of death and doom for all the Danes.
I saw the fire; the flames went flaring up.
They raced through rafters, roaring as they went,
Like winter wind, like storm-blown waves on rocks;
The light lit up all lands but did not last.
And then the roof and rafters crashed in ruins
While men stood by amazed and women mourned.

When daylight broke, the blaze had burned it all;
They searched the ashes seeking some remains,
A golden goblet or a bench still good.
1040 And in their hunt they found the horrid hand,
The grisly claw, of Grendel from the gable.
The hand had hung there at the highest point,
Unsoftened by the storms or summer sun
But forged to further hardness by the fire,
A weapon worse now than it was before;
The gold is gone but Grendel's claw remains.
It seems to be a symbol of our sorrows
For fire and foe have left us few and weak,
But evil somehow seems the stronger for it."
1050 King Hrethor halted, looking round the hall,
And said, "But now, my friend, I need to know
What sort of strength you bring to serve our cause.
Our forebears vowed a friendship for all time.
They pledged support; the need for it is plain.
You made your way here with your wives and young,
But Wittu says your ships brought soldiers too.
Your feud is with the Swedes; we fight the Franks.
Alone it seems most likely we would lose,
And yet our youth and unity bring strength;
1060 Let us makes vows of vengeance and win victory.
But Wiglaf said, "The women with me came
To seek your help, Lord Hrethor, in the hope
That ancient amity might open doors
For both our peoples, bound in brotherhood,
To look for and to learn new ways to live,
That all our families might be freed of fear.

Our stoutest men were slain by Swedish blades;
We want no wars to weaken us yet more.
Our sovereign, Beowulf, was strong yet steadfast,
1070 Not keen for combat if there could be peace.
The Scylfings saw no need to test his sword,
Contented to maintain a truce for years;
But when he died we dared adopt new ways
And Swedish blades drank up our bravest blood.
What good was that? What glory do we gain
By draining down our blood into the dust?
Do those in widow's weeds sing praise of war?
I stabbed a dragon when it scorched my shield
But dozing dragons cannot damage us;
1080 If Franks and Frisians are not fighting us,
Might we not let them live their lives in peace?
Come, Hrethor, help us now to heal these wounds.
We came here confident we could construct
A world where weak and strong might both live well
And people all might place their trust in peace."
Then Hrethor said, "I will not hide my heart
Which is most eager to distribute honor
To gallant scions of the glorious Geats;
No doubt the Danes are very much indebted
1090 To all who bear the blood of Beowulf
For daring deeds performed in other days,
But still we need to set a course ourselves
That looks at life now realistically,
So let us not conclude the case too quickly.
To those beside the ships food will be sent,
But I would ask that all now in our hall,

Strong warriors and worthy wives and children,
Remain with us to make their evening meal.
Let bards retell the tales of former triumphs,
1100   Of foes defeated and of friends sustained,
And I will call on careful counselors
To offer us advice." But Wiglaf answered,
"I'm sure, Lord Hrethor, that you seek to serve
Your people properly, improve their lives,
And not endanger any Danish dwelling.
You have a feud as well with foreign forces,
Marauding ranks who fell on you in wrath,
Whose hate-fire has turned Heorot to ashes.
But I have other ultimate concerns:
1110   A place of peace for people tired of war.
I think it best our band be at the boats
Prepared to push our prows away from shore,
Pursue our search with nations less concerned
With ancient injuries and harbored anger,
In lands and nations now unknown to us
Where feuds are few and folk are not oppressed
And righteousness bears rule throughout the realm."
King Hrethor, listening, laughed a little, asking,
"Do any nations know another way?"

1120   When darkness came, they did not join the Danes
To feast in fellowship or share their flagons
But stayed beside the ships and slept in tents.
When daylight drove the darkness from the heavens
The ravens roused them with their raucous cries
And Wiglaf sent the soldiers to the shore
To gather up the gear the Geats had brought

While women went to find their wandering children.
Then Hrethor sent his soldiers, saying to them,
"We must not let our friends take leave so lightly;
1130   Their arms would aid us greatly in the future."
But Wiglaf stood them off with spear and shield
Till they could drive their dragon boats from Denmark.
The sun in southern skies made bright the sea
As ring-prows, wind blown, made their westward way,
And followed swan-roads, skimming sea-gray waves.
The foam went flying as the sails unfurled;
The tall masts trembled and the timbers groaned
As prows kept plunging through the piling waves.
All day they sailed with Denmark in the distance;
1140   The sailors sometimes singing as they worked,
They hauled the high sails, heaved the steering oars,
As keels went cleanly through the ocean currents
And seagulls soared above the shifting breeze;
But women worried for their children's welfare
And how soon they might have another home
Where brides might come and babies could be born
And table food be shared and tales be told
And age be honored and the old might die
Amid the caring company of kin
1150   And folk might find an end at last to fear.

The third day they encountered thick white fog,
No sun, no shore, no sign that they could see,
A fog too thick to find a way to follow,
And silent, as the fog absorbed all sound;
A fog so thick it felt like winter fleece,
The sails hung slack, nor could the helmsmen steer

For lack of landmarks or a guiding light,
And so they spent the night still lost at sea.
When daylight dawned, the fog was driven off,
1160 The morning mist was melted by the sun,
And then they saw a shore with sandy beaches
And prows were pointed to approach the land;
They wanted water and were tired of waves.
The sailors ground their ships into the sand,
But mounted men came riding up, demanding
To know their nation and their names and purpose
And waving weapons. Wiglaf answered them,
"We have no nation nor are we renowned
For wielding weapons or for skill in war.
1170 We put in here, a place, so it appeared
Where we might find the water that we wanted."
The riders raised their weapons to be ready;
Their leader said, "Our lord has laid down rules
And ordered us to ask all unknown people
To leave at once, or wait beside the water
As captives while we call for more to come.
You must approach our prince as prisoners.
No stranger coming straight into our streets
Will have our help; these orders may seem harsh
1180 But safety is our chief and sole concern."
But Wiglaf said, "We will find water now;
So do withdraw your men and let us drink
And fill our empty water flagons first."
The spokesman, in response, drew back his spear
As if in anger, ominous to Wiglaf.
But Wiglaf drew his dagger, drove it deep

Into the horseman's side. He slowly slid
From horse to ground; the gore came gushing out
And stained the soil, a dark pool on the sand.
1190   The other riders rode off rapidly;
A horn was heard as if to call for help.
And Wiglaf said, "We will find water elsewhere."
They shoved the ships away from land and sailed
Along the coast but kept a watch for coves
Where they might seek for shelter safe from foes.
They found, before the evening came, a fjord
Whose sides fell steeply to the salty waves.
Tall pine trees stood, dark green against the ground,
And hemlock overhung the heaving waves
1200   That rose against the rocks around the edge.
A hawk was hovering high above the water
And circling slowly in the silent air.
They came to level land, a little bay;
A brook came bubbling down the bank
And grass was growing where some deer had grazed,
A pleasant scene. They pushed the prows ashore
And, leaping out, they lashed the boats to land.
The men then went to hunt, while women worked
To search for fuel and set up simple shelters
1210   And children ran in rings around the clearing.
The valiant men provided venison
To add to evening meals as daylight ended,
And then they settled safely down to sleep.

They woke to hear a scream so shrill and sad
It cut the quiet air, made blood run cold,
And left them troubled, trembling in their tents.

The soldiers reached to find their swords and shields;
Their eyes were open but the overcast
Had masked the moon above the mountaintops;
1220 They stumbled, searching, but they could not see
What kind of creature caused their blood to curdle.
When light returned at last, they looked and found
A man was missing from among their number,
A soldier known as Selfric, sturdy, brave,
Who feared no fight and never fled from battle.
A trail of blood led back into the brush;
Some footprints led them further in the forest,
But prints of such a size astounded them.
They knelt and noticed something none had known:
1230 The footprints felt like frost, but air was warm;
They would not follow further in the forest
But went to Wiglaf, wanting his advice.
He told them they should try to track them later,
And meanwhile make their campsite more secure.
They spent the day still settling in that spot;
It seemed an ideal site from every aspect:
The fjord full of fish, the woods with game,
The mountains making it remote from rivals
And sheltering the place from savage storms.
1240 Some men began to mark and measure out
Locations they would covet for a cabin
And places they could put a garden plot,
While women did their washing, watching children,
Concerned about the midnight screams and Selfric.
That night they built a bonfire, set it burning,
And picked and posted proven warriors,

Selected leaders who would spread alarms
If any sight or sound should startle them
Or any other outrage should occur
1250   Or strangers should approach the sleeping Geats.
Then all went off in order to find rest.
They were not sleeping well when once again
Such screams were heard as shook their very souls,
A horrid sound that hurt and chilled the heart.
The firelight gave a glimpse of ghastly beings,
As tall as trees and, terrible to see,
They grabbed the guards and ground them in their teeth.
Their eyes were green, but all the rest like ice,
A grayish tone that glistened in the gloom,
1260   Reflecting firelight from their frozen hearts.
The people, standing paralyzed in place,
Were frozen fast themselves in fear and dread.
The trolls kept taking others in their talons
And munching them to make their hideous meal.
Then Aelric, oldest, wisest of them all,
Said, "Trolls, I'm told, are terrified of fire."
So Wiglaf went directly to the watch fire
And seized a flaming faggot from the blaze
And, walking warily toward the trolls,
1270   He flung it squarely in the first one's face.
It burst abruptly as a bubble does
And left behind a little pool of liquid
Reflecting faintly the surrounding flames.
Then others also brandished burning branches
Until the trolls in terror fled away.
Then Wiglaf would have gone deep in the woods

And taken torches to attack the trolls;
He saw no reason to preserve the species.
But few would follow Wiglaf very far,
1280 So most remained amid their families
While Wiglaf and two other warriors went
To find the frozen phantoms in their lair.
They tracked the trolls, pursuing with no trouble
The frozen footsteps in the forest earth,
And came to cliffs where there were ancient caves;
In far-off times the trolls had taken them
From ogres who had always owned that land.
Within the cold, dark caverns trolls could keep
Their species from dissolving in the sun,
1290 And yet they had to hunt for human blood
Since none of them had any of their own.
The woeful creatures saw the comrades coming
And tore up forest trees to toss at them,
But they could hide unhurt behind some boulders
And then move forward from the forest screen
Because the trolls had turned and taken refuge
Within the caverns, cowering in their caves.
They broke dead branches off the trees to burn
And dropped them down the caverns' deep, black holes;
1300 The howls they heard showed some had hit their mark.
They sent down more and seething steam came out;
An awful odor almost overwhelmed them.
They stayed there till the sounds of sizzling ceased
And then returned again to tell in triumph
The saga of their sojourn, and the signs
That all their enemies were overcome

And peace might prove now to be possible.
That night the families feasted by the fire
And hailed the heroes who had shown such valor;
1310 They filled their flagons with the foaming ale
And joined in song and general jollity.
A bard sang sagas they had seldom heard
And let the lyre ring out its liquid music.
He told of how the trolls in ancient times,
When earth was cold and ice was everywhere,
Had crowned a king whose cavern deep in earth
Was ringed with rocks that had a radiance,
A glowing light that let them build their lives
In safety from the shining of the sun.
1320 The trolls were twice as tall as any man
And needed nothing for their nourishment
But ice, and oils that issued from the rock,
A timid, gentle tribe who never toiled
Or went to war; their wants were all supplied
Without an effort since their world's Creator
Had fully furnished all the folk would need.
And so for centuries, they never ceased
To pass their time in peace and so to prosper;
They kept their caverns with the utmost care,
1330 Embellished bountifully with brilliant jewels
Adorned with dignity and then bedecked
And finished in the very finest fashion.
But then a tempter talked to one young troll
About the beauties of the world above
Where there were fruits they had not found before
To touch and taste; the trolls knew only ice.

One night this troll ignored his nation's laws
To find a way into the wider world
And come again with glowing sun-warmed gifts.
1340   The trolls, entranced, returned and brought back more;
They lusted to enlarge their way of life
Though some assured them that the sun could kill.
Attracted by new treasures trolls rebelled;
They set aside the ancient style of life
And risked the sun's bright rays to reap its fruits.
The peaceful kingdom came to grief in chaos
As trolls attacked each other tooth and nail
And raided human regions for their riches;
They learned to like new liquids in their diet:
1350   The heat of human blood to warm their hearts.
This feud the trolls inflamed by fierce attacks
Until the terror of their tribe was told
With horror everywhere in human homes.
The bard kept singing sad and haunting songs;
Till all the ale was gone and ashes glowed
And firelight dwindled and the dew came down.

Next day they found some fragments in the forest,
The bits of human bone and body parts
Remaining from the meal the monsters made,
1360   And gathered them together in the glade.
They brought great beams and branches from the woods
And piled the pieces in a funeral pyre
To honor all whose flesh the trolls had eaten.
The smoke rose up and sorrow smote them all.

Then some of them were saying to themselves,
"We cannot build on land where bones are buried
Or make a home where heroes have been slain."
Still others ached for unforgotten homes
And some were sure that Wiglaf had destroyed
1370 Their lives and left them now with little hope
Of gold or glory, giving them no purpose.
They went to Wiglaf saying, "We must move
And search for some more suitable location,
A place of peace, as you have promised us,
Where families can flourish without fear
And all is guided by the gods for good.
You killed some trolls and all is clear and quiet
But maybe there are many more beyond,
Who lie there lurking in some lonesome place.
1380 Since some have fallen, all are filled with fear.
We only ask that we should now move on
To sandy shores or soaring peaks, but somewhere
Or anywhere at all that is not here."
But Wiglaf was not willing; he replied:
"I think that there is no place so unthreatening
It has no hardships we would have to face,
No place on earth that does not pose some perils.
And would you want no work that tests your skills,
Or choose to raise our children with no challenge?
1390 We may prefer to face a foreign foe,
But evil also lurks within ourselves;
I dread the danger lying deep within,
The foe we cannot often find or flee,
That swings no sword and throws no spear: the self.

So let us linger here a little longer
But send a single ship ahead to search
For pleasant places where we might have peace."
Then they selected Laefstan as their leader
And formed a company of fifteen fighters
1400 With skill as sailors, steadfast men of war,
And told them to return with truthful stories
About each area from every aspect:
The place, the people, and whatever prospect
They saw of settling there, constructing homes,
Of finding farmland, rivers full of fish,
Of raising children, rearing young folk rightly,
Of the inhabitants, and who were hostile,
Indeed, of every danger to a dwelling
And every asset to an honest life.
1410 So then they stocked a ship with spears and swords
In case they came upon a hostile country,
And various provisions for the voyage,
And set out then to seek a place of safety.
They fared forth from the fjord they had found
And north through waters new, unknown, to them.
They sailed up fjords, found defenseless towns,
And plundered people, pillaged as they went,
And gathered up the gold, neglecting nothing
That caught their fancy, making fearful figures;
1420 The natives fled before them and their fury
While ravens, black-clad birds of battlefields,
Came flocking down to follow them and feast
On carrion corpses killed and left behind.
So when they sailed back south the ship was laden

With riches robbed from all throughout the region;
They sailed exulting in their great success
And hoping they would have a hero's welcome.
Meanwhile their comrades, careful carpenters,
Had built with boards and heavy, oaken beams
1430 Some strong but simple shelters in the clearing
The soldiers had been sent to search for food
And brought deer back and several kinds of birds;
They smoked and salted some and ate the rest.
Each night they set a sentry for their safety,
Arranged a ring of fires around their camp,
But still they failed to find refreshing rest.
The memory of missing men was strong,
And some of them woke screaming from their sleep;
The dread of death intruded on their dreams.
1440 They watched as well to see the warriors
Returning from their travels; they would try
To see explorers sailing up the fjord.
The soldiers sent to scout the land ahead,
The comrades, came back down the Norway coast;
They found the fjord they had started from
And sailed their ship past cliffs of slanting rock
To make their landing. Laefstan led his crew
To bring their boat into the stony beach
Where comrades clustered round them, questioning:
1450 "Where have you been? What booty have you brought?"
For some could see the treasure in the ships.
But Wiglaf asked: "What are you bringing us?
What land is lying out there which is like
The homes we had and which we hope to have?"

And Laefstan said, "The lands we learned about
Cannot oppose our prowess. We made peace
With sword and spear and brought back their possessions
To deck our dwellings with this dazzling wealth.
We found no folk with strength to stand before us
1460   Or keep us from acquiring all their country;
The gods enabled us to gain much glory."
Then Wiglaf asked, "And is this all you did?
You found some feeble people in the forest
And slaughtered them and stole from them their substance
And so you speak of peace. You silenced all
Your victims' voices with your violence
And tell us tales of what you now call triumph.
But now the coasts of Norway, near and far,
Will be alert, on guard against the Geats;
1470   Indeed, I dread the doom you bring on us
As others everywhere will seek us out
To wipe away the memory of your war
And punish us, your people, for their pain."

Then Laefstan in his anger answered Wiglaf,
"But look what we have lost with you as leader:
Our hearths, our homes, and all our happiness.
It's time we Geats should go to war again
And brighten rusted blades with steaming blood
Until the tribes around us learn to tremble
1480   And we regain the glory that is gone."
But Wiglaf's words were warm with indignation:
"What good is gold and glory without peace?
What future can you fetch us with your fame?"
Then Laefstan called his comrades, bade them come

And stand with him and strive as soldiers should.
But Aelric asked him, "Is this how the Geats
Have learned to act in loyalty to their leaders?"
Would you win glory setting Geat on Geat?"
But Laefstan lunged at Aelric with his lance
1490   And hit him in the heart with his full strength;
The thrust went through his body, thin and old,
And brought the blood out, spurting from his back.
He fell down on his face at Laefstan's feet.
Undaunted, Wiglaf drew his dagger out
And called on those with courage, bade them come
And face him fairly if they felt like Laefstan.
But Laefstan stood alone. He looked for help
And found that there were few who were his friends,
For Aelric was an elder held in honor;
1500   It grieved the Geats to see him in his gore.
Then someone threw a spear, assaulting Laefstan,
That landed just below his linden shield
And gashed his groin. Again a spear came flying
That hit below his helmet; he fell down
To earth and lost his life. So Laefstan died
As Wiglaf sought a way to stop the slaughter.
He said, "This killing of ourselves must cease;
We are too few to fight." He faced them down
And brought about an end before a battle,
1510   A test between the two sides, could occur.
He ordered them to act in unity
And not to hurt their hope to find a haven
Where folk could flourish free at last of fear.
Again he gave command to go for wood

And build a pyre on which to burn the bodies.
Some murmured that they might have made two pyres
A lesser one for Laefstan lest it seem
That he and Aelric earned an equal honor;
But Wiglaf wanted all to be as one
1520 And not divide a victim and a victor
Since death, he said, was still the same for all.
Then folk went out to forage in the forest
And bring the branches back to build the pyre.
They took the treasure and contributed
The helms and hauberks and the hilted swords
The golden goblets, wonderfully engraved,
And other objects, torn from those who owned them,
And placed the costly pieces on the pyre,
A tribute to the two whose lives were taken.
1530 Then Wiglaf spoke some words to them in wisdom:
"We honor all who died, but Aelric more,
Whose careful counsel we have counted on;
He went on board the boat with Beowulf
To meet the monster many years ago,
And heard King Hrothgar speak of heroes,
About the doom death brings to all who breathe.
'A short time,' said he, 'yes, and all too soon
Will sword and sickness come to sap your strength
Or fangs of fire or else the surging flood
1540 Or sting of sword or else the spear in flight
Or agonies of age or else the eye,
Now dazzling, dims and darkens; all too soon
Will death, O warrior, work its will with you.'
So Hrothgar said, but is there something still

We need to know, or is there nothing more?
We piled our presents on the funeral pyre
As evidence of honor they have earned,
But this is only fuel to feed the flames.
The gold we glean today is gone tomorrow,
1550   And yet we yearn for something far beyond
These riches that will only rust and rot;
Our greed can never gain a lasting good
Nor fame, that also fails and fades with time,
For men are mortal, memories are short,
And we forget the glory that was gained.
The deeds we do, however, will endure
And form the future for our families;
Society is shaped by our decisions.
So Laefstan's lust becomes his legacy
1560   While Aelric's wisdom is a gift to all
To guide the Geats wherever they may go."
He stopped, unsure his sermon had been heard;
"But now, he said, "the night is coming near
And we have work for all with willing hands,
So take your torches to the waiting pyre
And let us burn the bodies of the brave
To honor all whose lives were joined with ours."
They fetched the fire and soon the flames leaped up,
A searing sister of the noonday sun,
1570   That melted in its heat the men's remains;
They saw the bone-cage broken in the blaze.
The Geats stood gazing till the fire was gone

And ash alone was left of two men's lives,
Then made their evening meal with mournful hearts.

That night another troll came near their camp;
It seemed that they were sensitive to smells
And came from far to find the human flesh
Whose burning smell was borne them on the breeze.
The troll had talons terrible to see
1580 And eyes that glowed a ghastly greenish hue;
The troll attempted to attack the camp
But fearing fire it whimpered fretfully
And broke off branches blundering through the forest.
At last it came too close and quickly burst,
Collapsing in a little pool of liquid
That sizzled slightly in a sudden wind.

Next morning many women made their way
To Wiglaf wanting time for words with him.
The troll attack had terrified them all;
1590 They could not feel secure in such a country.
The warriors thought that speaking was unworthy
And seemed to show too much uncertainty,
But they were thankful that the women's thoughts
Should be expressed. They were not bold to block them.
Then Wiglaf said he sympathized, but still,
"No place on earth is perfect; peace is rare.
And if we found a land with fewer fears
Where sleeping dragons did not seem to dwell
And trolls had not been told of till this time,
1600 Where fields are fair and forest full of game,
A place where people have not put their mark,

With shattered shields and broken spears and lances,
Yes, if there is an island without people,
Whose shores are still unstained by human blood,
It will not stay that way if we are there.
We learned from Laefstan what our hearts are like
And changing homes can hardly change the heart."
But Yrfa, Wiglaf's wife, said, "We agree;
Yet logic all alone is little use
1610   When hearts are hungry and the hearth is cold.
We only know we ache for inner peace,
To see our children safe beneath the sun;
We have been hurt too much to call this home."

Then Wiglaf sent for sages, senior men,
Who by their careful counsel could assist
In thinking through what things they ought to do
And helping him decide how he should act.
The first to speak was Fredgar, fond of fighting
And proud of his opinions and appearance;
1620   He said, "We should go home and do it soon;
We do not need to dwell with danger here.
This fjord feels to me like foreign soil;
I am too old to understand new ways.
In Geatland we were well established once,
With hearths and homes and good, familiar habits,
And even enemies we understood.
It was not wise to leave our homes to wander;
It will be best if we go back, rebuild,
And let our children grow again as Geats."
1630   Then Siric spoke, a seasoned warrior,
And one of two who tracked the trolls with Wiglaf.

"It seems to me," he said, "we should remain;
Why should we seek to face the Swedish swords
That killed so many of our closest comrades?
I fear not for myself, but some will fall,
And wives will wait to hear that they are widows.
I am too old to look for enemies;
This is a peaceful, pleasant kind of place,
Well sheltered from the stress of violent storms.
1640 The forests can be cleared for fertile fields,
A rich array of wildlife roams the woods,
The fjord flowing by abounds in fish,
And if the trolls are troublesome at times,
A blazing branch will quickly beat them off.
So let us stay where we are settled now
And move no more until we truly must."

The oldest of them all was Ethelbyrht,
A warrior well regarded for his wisdom;
He spoke more slowly, but with certainty:
1650 "Not much remains of all that we remember;
The past is ashes, yes, and even if
We go to live in Geatland once again
And build anew what now lies burned and broken,
It will not work for us as once it did.
The circling sun cannot be sent back east;
No yearning yields our yesterdays again.
And we are not the same as once we were.
A life untroubled by the trolls is tame
And yet we should not simply seek excitement
1660 Or linger long where trolls are known to lurk.
I am uneasy in this area;

I think we cannot quite be comfortable
Where deadly danger is a daily threat.
I am not fond of fleeing out of fear
But we are wives as well as warriors;
Our goal must be the good of all the Geats.
Yet if we are not able to remain,
I favor moving forward for our future,
To look for lands where we can live in peace
1670 Until our tribe attains a larger size
And we can once again go out to war
And let the foreign people feel our fury
And garner glory for ourselves, the Geats."
The other soldiers shouted their assent;
They wanted war but saw the need to wait
Until the time when they could gain more treasure.
They had not heard of heavenly rewards
Nor did they rightly see how riches rot,
How little good is glory in the grave.

1680 Then Wiglaf, son of Weohstan, chose words
And spoke with calm and quiet confidence;
Avoiding conflict, he unveiled his vision,
The hope he held to of a peaceful haven:
"The search that we are on is still the same:
Behind or yet ahead, we seek a home,
But words are weak; no one of us can say
In measured words what means the most to us
Or paint the picture prized within our hearts.
It is what some have seen in battle-strife:
1690 The courage then required amid the killing.
It is what some see staying safe inside:

The babies bawling while the kettle boils.
It is what some will see in country scenes:
The trees they treasure and the tors they know.
And some have seen it in the search itself,
Who hang their hopes upon a distant hill
Yet relish more the route than the arrival.
But let us go together toward our goal
And step by step see what its shape may be.
1700   Our children have their choice of challenges
But we must find our way and go as one
To find the future of the Geats as friends.
So come, my comrades, act with courage now
And someday bards will sing about our sojourn."
Then Wiglaf said that soldiers should assemble
Their arms and armor, place them in the boats
While other people should prepare supplies,
Should fill the flagons, and should gather food,
Should bake more loaves and bring them all on board;
1710   And some should sew the sails that had been torn,
And paint the prows in colors proud and bright,
And make new masts if any might be broken.
Still others Wiglaf asked to mend the oars
And see that they were smoothly shaped and sound.
Those skilled in hunting he sent out in haste
To find what fowl or other flesh they could
And bring it back to be prepared to take.
A few brought fish and fruit that had been dried.
Some brought fresh roots and berries to the boats;
1720   Still others cooked and cleaned and carried
Whenever others asked them to assist.

In two short days they did these various duties.
The final night they feasted by the fire
And told each other tales of weary travels,
The stories told by some and sung by others.
The bard embellished them as best he could
And sang old songs long stored up in his mind;
He made new words for many he remembered,
Entwining them so he could tell new tales.
1730 And sang of princes placed in hateful peril
In other lands where ogres eat men whole
And then he sang of Scyld, the son of Scef,
Who, though without a home, an orphan, outcast,
A foundling, taught his foes to fear his name
And grew to win great glory, glowing fame.
He sang of Scyld's son, Beow, brave in battle,
And his son, Halfdane, high king after him.
Then Halfdane's son, called Hrothgar, held the throne
And he it was who built the hall called Heorot,
1740 So fine a place its fame had spread afar,
Though of it only ashes now remain.
The fire was dying down, the song was done,
And soldiers went to seek a place to sleep.

When morning came and men and women moved,
The sun's rays sparkled on the shining water
And all things were as in its Author's plan.
Then some were gloomy, others glad to go.
The last of their belongings were collected
And carried, clothes and food and cooking pots,
1750 To stow them safely on the waiting ships.
Then Wiglaf sent the soldiers out to search

Throughout the area for anything
Of value on their voyage or their venture.
They searched the ground and all the simple shelters
But all were empty, nothing anywhere.
So Wiglaf ordered ships to set their sails;
They lifted leather sails along the masts,
All brightly painted, brilliant blue and red.
A fresh breeze through the fjord followed them
1760   And set the ripples racing round the ships.
They gazed again at granite walls of rock
And falls of broken stones that faced the fjord
And watched the wind begin to whip up waves.
The current carried them along the coast,
Then out at last into the open ocean.
The line of land grew lower as they watched;
They left behind the hemlock-covered hills
And headed toward the west as Wiglaf wanted.
The billow-riders bore them bravely on.
1770   At last they were alone; no land in sight.
The women watched for serpents warily;
The men were more intent on seeing mermaids.
But all was calm; the sea was smooth and still
With just the faintest froth of lacy foam.
The ships were sliding smoothly on the waves.
The sailors watched the sun and steered due west;
At night they needed skies with not a cloud
So they could set their steering by the stars.
Thus on they went, still working to the west.

1780   The second day, a storm came from the south.
At first they felt a freshening of the breeze,

Then clouds were coming up to cloak the sky.
It was midday, but still the darkness deepened;
The wind began to grow with stronger gusts,
And then a clap of thunder threatened them.
The children cried and cowered under covers
While sailors strove to strike the flapping sails
Before a blast would break the bending masts.
The rain came small and soft at first, in spurts,
1790   But harder then, like hail, that hit with force,
Till rain was running down their clothes in rivers
And they were soaked and sodden with the spray.
Their clothes grew clammy with the cold and wet;
The salty sea-spray stung against their skin.
The wind was raging, rising to a roar,
Till they could hardly hear above the howling;
It drove them on, half drowned and drenched.
They shook and shivered in the savage cold.
The rolling billows wrenched their narrow rafts
1800   And boats were bending on the billows' crests,
The ring-prows rolling in the rising waves
And windblown water washing over them.
The sailors said they had not seen such waves
That heaved and hurtled down on them like hills.
The steering oars of some ships snapped in two;
To point the prows became impossible
And surely, Wiglaf thought, some ships would sink
Unless some help should happen from on high.
That night and next day too they knew no change;
1810   The swirling storm raged still in all its fury,
While sleepless sailors sought to stay afloat

And breaking seas still beat upon their barks.
They had no sun or stars by which to steer
Nor hope they might behold their homes again.
The next night came; the sea surge seemed to slacken.
The storm swell ceased to surge against the boats;
The dreadful wind was dying down at last.
The fourth day dawned and finally the fleet
Could ride the rolling waves with restful ease;
1820   The black and brooding clouds were breaking up,
And soon a warming sun was shining down.
The children crept out from their cloaks and coverings
And women went to work to look through baggage
To find some food to put in famished mouths.
So now they knew once more which way was north;
They hauled up heavy sails and headed west,
Though all the boats were badly mauled and battered
With splintered masts and shattered steering oars.
They sought a place to put in for repairs,
1830   A landing to relax and have some leisure,
For they were tired of tumult and of tossing,
More weary of the waves than words could tell.

As dusk came down, they saw a distant land
But Wiglaf wisely ordered them to wait
And sail in circles till the sun came up;
There could be danger driving on in darkness
Of wrecking all their ships on rocks and reefs,
And if they sought to sleep on unknown shores,
Their foes might fall on them before they knew
1840   What type of tactics would protect them best.
The moon had set; the sky was full of stars,

And Wiglaf, wakeful, wondered why it was
That stars in every land are still the same.

When first the flush of dawn spread from the east
They slowly sailed the ships toward the land;
The bright sails billowed in the early breeze.
They watched for signs of life: a sentry stationed,
A farmer in a field, or fishermen,
Or smoke ascending from a single house.
1850 They heard the curlews' cry and seagulls' calling
But neither sight nor sound of human source.
The water went between low hills and widened
To bring them to a broad and spacious bay
Where many seals were sleeping on the shore,
A peaceful place where people might live well;
Yet still they saw no sign of human life
Until they traveled to a certain point
Around a narrow neck of land and knew
They were not first to find this far-off place,
1860 Though still they saw no sentinel on guard
Or any evidence of other people
Except some boats abandoned on the beach
As if some fisher folk had fled away.
So Wiglaf let them land to look around
And search beyond the shore for something more.
Behind some hillocks, they discovered homes
Where they were sheltered from the sea and storms.
The people there were poor and living peacefully
In shelters made of stone, with roofs of sod.
1870 They welcomed Wiglaf's warriors as friends
And offered them some other, unused land

Where they could feel quite free to farm;
They had no taste for any type of trouble.
The Geats were glad to go ashore and rest
But wished to wait, conferring with each other,
Before deciding if the site was suitable.
The natives noticed that their guests would need
To find some water and sufficient food.
They showed them near the ships a bubbling spring
1880   And also showed them herbs that they could eat
And certain kinds of seaweed for a soup.
They said the land they lived on was not linked
To any other land; it was an island,
And occupied by peasants, poor as they,
With other islands all around their own,
And hamlets huddled here and there throughout,
And farmers growing grain and raising goats.
But wealth and warfare were not known among them.

Then Wiglaf ordered off an expedition
1890   To go and get some greater sense about
The island and its opportunities,
To try to find some unused fertile fields
And seek a sheltered place in which to settle
At least a little longer, days or weeks,
And so replenish food supplies and plan
A course of action all agreed upon.
Then, meanwhile, most of those remaining,
Awaiting this report, would work with Wiglaf
Rebuilding battered boats as best they could

1900   And sorting out the stuff that had been spoiled
By waves and water washing over them.

The chosen warriors went away at once
And strode back into camp as sun was setting
Quite pleased and proud to come again with presents:
A goat which they had gotten as it grazed
Was slung beneath a spear two soldiers carried,
While others brought two otters and some eels
Which they had speared while standing by a stream.
They also said that they had seen strange sights:
1910   A hill not made by any human hands,
A massive mound that had amazed them all,
And stones beyond the might of men to move
That stood on end and stretched toward the sky.
They thought it might be magic that had moved them
But also wondered whether once there was
A race of giants who could wrest such rocks,
The standing stones that made them stop and stare.
The mound they saw had made them all imagine
A dragon's treasure trove with wealth untold
1920   Was stored up secretly and deep inside
There must be golden goblets well engraved
And sharp-edged swords wrought with the skill of elves
And shining banners brilliantly embroidered
And other articles once owned by men
But buried by some bygone race of heroes
And even now unknown and quite unnoticed.
They said that they had searched for some way in
But boulders far too big had blocked their way.
Then Wiglaf asked, "What is it ails you all?

1930   Why must I now remind you of the meeting
       That brought a baleful death to Beowulf,
       The fatal fire that fell on many houses,
       Because a robber raised the dragon's wrath?
       You were not willing to reward him then,
       Allot your leader loyalty in his need,
       And stand beside him when the serpent struck.
       And would you risk arousing all the wrath
       That such a serpent might now spend on you?
       There is no time to waste on tales of treasure
1940   When we have work still waiting to be done."

       But day by day, when duties were assigned,
       The soldiers who were sent to scout out game
       To feed their families always found the time,
       When they had speared some sleeping seals,
       To dig and delve, work downward in the mound,
       Until one tumbled through into a space,
       An empty room lined all around with rock,
       And nothing buried there but broken bones.
       In anger then, they asked who else had come
1950   In former times to take the dragon's treasure.
       And so they scratched their runes into the stone
       And let the letters tell of those they loved;
       They made their marks for other men to see
       And then they sealed the sepulcher with sod
       And went away but did not talk to Wiglaf
       About the buried bones they had discovered.

       But meanwhile other searching soldiers saw
       Some hillocks here and there that had them puzzled.

Not far beneath the sod were slabs of stone
1960 That seemed to cover caves or crevices.
The natives said they knew the grassy knolls
Or hollow hills were now the homes of draugrs,
The dwellings of the dead; they dreaded them.
Especially when the days were short, they shivered,
If hurrying home they had to pass such hills
For then the draugrs did such dreadful deeds
As filled the country folk with nameless fear.

For weeks the people passed the time in peace,
Assembling shelters from the stone and sod
1970 And finding food, both fish and game, to eat.
And yet they all seemed ill at ease and restive;
The country made them quite uncomfortable
In some uncertain way. They were not sure
They really could arrange to put down roots
And make their homes amid these hollow hills
In dread of draugrs and in constant doubt;
What hope could hold them in this haunted island?
They went to Wiglaf to discuss these worries.
"I have been hoping," Herbrund said, "to find
1980 A land to live in that is lacking nothing
A farmer needs to shape a family's future.
I think this country cannot quite provide
The assets I would ask for in a home;
I think the soil is thin, the clouds too thick,
There are no trees to take for timber
Or fell for fuel or build a fire for warmth.
The brush and bracken that they burn
Will hardly cook our food or heat our homes.

I miss the sun-filled meadows and the mountains;
1990   I would prefer to find a fairer land
And sometime soon, before the summer ends."
And for the first time Fredgar felt the same:
"There is no future for us in these islands.
I see no glory to be gained or gold
Among these peasants; people here are poor
In war and wealth and knowledge of the world.
There is no fame to find in fighting them,
To kill or conquer them wins no acclaim.
The warrior's way is not to watch the weather,
2000   Appointing times to plow and plant and reap,
And using spears to set upon a seal;
I would not stay here eating eggs and oysters
If there is work for warriors in the world."
The warriors slammed their spears against their shields
Applauding Fredgar's words. They felt that fighting,
The clash of combat, comrades at one's side,
The bucklers breaking as they bear the impact
Of swinging swords and lethal spears in flight,
The hammer blows on hardened, hand-linked rings,
2010   And shimmer of the sun on shining armor,
Indeed, the death that is a warrior's doom,
Was better far at last than being buried
In such a placid, peaceful place as this.
Then others also spoke their minds; they uttered
Their varied viewpoints, vying to be heard.
Some seemed to think a southern route was safer,
Some wanted to explore a westward way,
Some sought a better soil and others strife,

But most were of one mind, that they should move,
2020 And looked to Wiglaf to select as leader
A future course on which they could concur.

Then Yrfa, wife of Wiglaf, spoke for women;
She said, "Our search has gone on for a season
But has not, here or elsewhere, found a home,
A place where we can plant our crops in peace;
This island also is not what we seek,
But life's too short to spend it all on ships
So let us look for open, fertile land—
Not perfect, that's not possible, but proper—
2030 We simply need enough for normal life,
The safe and simple things that satisfy,
And near enough that no more people die."
Then Wiglaf said, "I do not want to wander
Or travel all the time; we truly must
Stop roaming soon, arrive where we can rest.
But now we need to look a little longer
Until the Sovereign shows us where to settle,
Almighty Maker of the Middle Earth,
The place appointed in his purposes
2040 For us to occupy and end our journey."

So Wiglaf ordered all to act at once
To bring their baggage to the boats again,
Sufficient food for every family,
Assemble all on board the ships to sail.
Then Wiglaf asked the islanders' for insight
In looking for a land where they might live,

A course they could pursue with confidence,
To sites more suitable for settlement.

They said they knew of nothing to the north
2050 Except some barren islands, bleak and bare
And washed by waves and constant, savage winds;
Still further north were islands all of ice
Where none would like to linger very long.
They thought the west led out to endless ocean
Where monsters, they imagined, made their home.
But there were certain sea-paths to the south,
That offered other opportunities.
To those who dared, undaunted, all the dangers.
They said a larger land was lying there
2060 With massive mountains that no man could climb,
Where snow was often seen and stinging cold.
They said the mountain folk were few but fierce;
They told of tribes so wild and turbulent
Their bitter feuds were famous far away—
A hateful, hostile, cruel, unconquered country
But one with running rivers rife with fish
And crowded forests full of deer and pheasants.
They also told him travelers had returned
To say that they had seen a writhing serpent
2070 That captured ships and crushed them in its coils
And snapped up sailors, swallowing them whole.
This monster made its home among the mountains,
In glens where none dared go without a guide.
But further south, they said, were softer lands
With kinder climate and a gentle coast.
They had not seen this countryside themselves;

The hazards they had heard of left no hope
Of reaching other regions at such risk.
But Wiglaf did not take the time to talk
2080 With others, asking elders their opinions.
It seemed to him that sailing to the south
Was now the only option if they hoped
To find a final refuge fairly soon.
So Wiglaf mustered all the men, commanded
Equipment be secured and cargo stowed
And all the ships be set to sail at once.
The breeze that backed them as they left the bay
Encouraged them and kept them on their course.
The standing stones were clearly to be seen,
2090 A sight that overwhelmed them all with awe,
Amazed when they imagined giants moving
And shaping stones of such colossal size;
But they were thankful that they had not met
The makers of the massive monument
And had not stayed where some might set upon them.
Beyond the bay they entered open ocean;
Waves crashed against the coastal cliffs behind
And rocked the ring-prowed ships with rolling billows.
The shifting clouds obscured the sun; the wind
2100 Was whipping white waves up along the whale road
But still the sailors kept their course due south,
A heading that they hoped would have success
And lead them to the land for which each longed.
It seemed a short time passed until they saw
A line of land below a bank of clouds,
And then a high and harsh and rocky headland

With rocks that ringed the base, and raging waves
That beat against the barrier; no boat
Could hope to find a harbor without harm
2110   In such a surf. The sailors shifted course
And drifted down the coast throughout the day
But did not land for fear of finding foes.
As day was drawing to a close, they did
Observe a bay, a somewhat sheltered cove,
And steered their ships in through the pounding surf.
A river ran down falling over rocks
And splashing softly in the sunless sea.
The shore was swampy and not suitable
To stay; too little of the land was level.
2120   They bound the boats to stakes as best they could
And let some land but left the rest on board.
For several days they sailed still further south
While clinging closely to the rocky coast
And stopping sometimes to refresh themselves
And look for food and fill their flagons.
At times the sailors tried to terrify
The children saying they had seen a serpent;
The boys were gleeful, but the girls began
To cry and cower while the sailors cackled.

2130   One sunset, as they drew the ships to shore
And gathered goods together for a meal,
Attending to their tasks, they were attacked
And suddenly assailed by savages
Who had no armor, only bows and arrows,
But sent their shafts with horrifying skill;
Some fell before they fully realized

That they were even threatened. Thick and fast
The arrows came at them, and quickly killed
Two warriors and one among the women.
2140 The soldiers swiftly reached for spears and swords,
Their helmets, and their hardened, hand-linked hauberks
To face the phantoms shooting from the forest,
The unseen enemy whose lethal arrows
Were raining down around them as they ran.
The battle-tempered soldiers bent their bows
To shoot but could not see the arrows' source,
Concealed and shrouded by the sheltering trees.
The shining armor-plate impeded progress;
Their chain mail checked them as they tried to charge
2150 Into the trees and tripped on tangled roots.
The brush and branches blocked their bold advance
And helped the hostile horde within the woods.
Then Wiglaf went himself into the woods
And with no bulky armor on was able,
Protected by the trees, to test his sword
Against the unseen, ghostly gladiators,
And swinging, stabbing, send them reeling back.
Then Waelric, one of Waelstan's stalwart sons,
The tallest of that tough and hardy tribe,
2160 And one of those who went with Wiglaf
With burning branches to attack the trolls,
When he had seen the way that Wiglaf worked,
Took up his sword and set out in the same way
To find their foe and put them all to flight.
Attempting to protect himself with trees,
He forced his way still further in the forest

And battered bowmen with his blood-soaked sword,
Unable to take aim as he rushed on them;
He drove them down before they drew their bows
2170   And left the landscape littered with their bodies.
The moon emerged from melancholy clouds
And shone down on a scene of pain and sorrow.
They brought thick branches from the woods to burn,
A funeral pyre prepared for those who perished;
The smoke ascended in the silent sky
While watchers wept and all bewailed their loss.
The Geats kept guard that night against attack
In fear the furtive bowmen who had fled
Might come in quest of all their fallen comrades
2180   With further forces furious at their loss.
When sunlight came the soldiers set about
The task of taking food and tools and armor
And bearing it on board the waiting boats.
The comrades clearly could not linger there
Or hope to make a home in hostile land.
But Wiglaf told them, "We were amply warned
That perils would appear along this path
And dangers, as indeed they did last night,
But we have set ourselves a certain purpose
2190   And have agreed to work to gain that goal
And find what fate affords us, fair or foul.
The world still turns, and testing times will come
Along the road, till we arrive, and reach
The promised place for those who persevere.
The mist-filled mountains are diminishing
The high-born eagles' home and haunt of wolves;

The land is lower now, and I believe
The end of all our travels is approaching."
Once more they slipped their moorings, raised their masts,
2200   And set their course toward the southern sun.

The Geats, still gloomy, still engaged in mourning,
Were saddened by the sight of sullen clouds
That quickly cast a curtain on the sun
And hid the land ahead behind a veil.
The people never noticed now the sting of salt
Or how the wash of water wet their clothes.
The mists that made them miserable before,
The constant cold, the crowding in the boat,
Were almost easy now to overlook;
2210   The weary world they knew was always wet.
So on they went and envied other people
Who stood on solid ground and saw their lives
As fixed and felt no doubts about the future.

At last they saw an island, lying low,
With cabins crudely crafted out of stone,
A shallow harbor on the sheltered side
Protected well against the wind and waves,
And brought their boats together in the bay.
On coming closer, they could clearly see—
2220   Amazed—those moving on the isle were men;
There were no women, and they wondered why.
It seemed that some essential element
Was lacking in the lives these people lived.
They wondered, too, why not a one had weapons.
They had no arms; there was no armor on them.

They seemed to feel quite safe in their surroundings,
As if they had no enemies at all.
These men came out to meet them as they moored
And answered easily the questions they were asked:
2230   They claimed to come from countries to the west
And said their style of life was set by some
Who gave up everything they owned on earth
To find a treasure better far than fame,
A gift they said was greater far than gold.
The people practiced poverty and prayer;
They had no wealth and waged no wars
But tried to teach the children trusted to them
To write and read and mumble prayers by rote.
They looked for poor and isolated lands
2240   To pass their time in peace apart from those
Whose lives were ruled by greed, whose goal was gain.
Then Wiglaf asked them other questions also
And stood there on the shore in conversation
While all about him people beached their boats
And waited, wondering what they were to do.
So Waelric spoke to Wiglaf sharply saying,
"You cannot take the time now just to talk;
When folk are hungry, feeding them comes first,
And then comes time for those who wish to think."
2250   "Why eat," said Wiglaf, "if you cannot ask?
To live is not worth much unless you learn;
The mind needs meat as much as does the mouth."
But then he laughed and led them to unload
Sufficient for a few days on the island;
By now he knew that there was not enough

To hold them here where soldiers could not hunt
Or farmers find a place to plow and plant.
The Geats could well have gone again next day
But Wiglaf hoped to have more time to hear
2260 About the peaceful, brown-robed brotherhood
Who said they served a single, unseen God
And lived in loyalty to God alone.
They said their style of life was very simple;
They did not wish to waste time worrying
About the realm of things that rot and rust
But sought instead a country less uncertain,
An everlasting life they longed for now.
To gain this wisdom, Wiglaf was prepared
To stay with them and seek to understand.
2270 No tongue had told him of the true Creator,
The God who governs all things for our good;
He longed to linger on the island learning
The message that these men had made their own.
But Waelric warned him others would not wait,
That many of the men were murmuring
That even loyalty at last has limits.
Then Wiglaf asked in anger whether any
Remembered how, not many months before,
The loyalty they owed their lord was lacking;
2280 They did not crowd around our king in crisis.
The dragon's fire and fury set them fleeing
And some were sent to exile to their shame;
No happiness of home and hearth is theirs.
"Go tell those troublemakers to be brave,
And sit in silence while I seek advice.

Our friends here travel frequently and far
And know this coast and can provide good counsel.
They tell me if we travel two more days
That we will come to cliffs along the coast
2290   With headlands high above the heaving waves
And reach a river running to the sea
And forming there a harbor full of fish.
Above the sea the brotherhood has built
A place of prayer where they can live in peace;
And side by side there is a sisterhood
Where women also walk that way of life.
They say that we would surely be received
And welcomed warmly as we go our way.
And they have just suggested that we journey
2300   Beyond that point till we approach a place
Where fields stretch flat as far one can see.
They say that we could sail there in our ships
By keeping constantly upon our course
In six or seven days without a storm.
The place they picture seems to be appealing,
Because the fields are fertile and are full
Of streams that sailing ships could use with ease.
So we could make our home amid the marshes,
Well hidden from all harm and hostile folk,
2310   And find the food we need by clearing farms,
But still could seek provisions on the sea.
Perhaps some clans now camping there will claim
The land is theirs and thrust at us and threaten,
And force our fighters to be firm with them,
And give them work to do to gain some glory.

And will our war-starved warriors be pleased
To do their duty if that day should come?
But all this I have learned while seeming idle;
There is a time to talk and pay attention
2320 To men familiar with the many miles
Of landscape lying now along our way.
But now we know these things we need to move;
It seems to me that we should sail as soon
As your array of restless folk are ready."
So once again they gathered all the Geats
And told them that the time had come to travel,
But now they knew the nature of the journey
And could be clear about the course ahead:
No doubt there would be danger every day
2330 But at the end a home for all of them.

They packed the ring-necked prows with their supplies
And bade good-bye to all the brotherhood,
Who promised to support them with their prayers.
The sprays of water sparkled as they sped,
And hearts were high with thoughts of finding home.
A willing wind was with them all that day;
The billow-rider, banners in the breeze,
Sped fast and fleet across the rolling foam.
That night they came upon a quiet cove
2340 And sheltered there with sentries stationed round,
But none came near, annoying them that night.
The women dreamed of daily chores and duties
And sharing meals among familiar friends
In homes where hearths were hallowed by long use;
And young men visioned valiant victories

As soldiers slew their foes in fierce assault,
And others' dreams were filled with fertile fields
And growing grain that gleams in summer sun.
They did not dream of distant, unknown shores,
2350   But only of what they had always known:
Familiar things were what they missed the most
And hoped to have again to heal their hearts.
They woke to find a fog that filled the cove,
As thick as new-laid thatch; it held them there
A second day till they could see to sail.

The heaven-ruler, robed in clouds, arose
And sent them scattered showers as they sailed,
But wet no longer worried weary travelers;
The dreamt-of destination drove them on
2360   Across the constant cresting of the waves.
The puffs of wind propelled the painted sails
Until they reached the region of the river,
And turning toward the tall cliffs flanking it
They saw some simple shelters on the ness
Along the river's southern side and saw,
Above them on the bank, the brownish robes
That marked the men whom they had met before.
But here there were some women wearing them
Because this colony included both;
2370   The men and women met at certain moments,
Appearing at appointed times for prayer,
But staying otherwise in separate shelters.
The boats were brought upriver to a beach
And sentries set to guard the ships from harm;
Then Wiglaf went, and with him several others,

To climb the cliff and meet the comrades there.
The Geats brought greetings from the northern group
And took some tokens to be recognized
And offered them as evidence of honor.
2380　The members met them, made them very welcome,
Politely led the Geats to find their leader,
A well-known woman, honored for her wisdom,
Whose name was Hilda. Having traveled here
From Lindisfarne to found this fellowship,
She gathered in a growing group of folk
Who sought a stable center for their lives,
A place of order in an unruled world.
She welcomed Wiglaf and his comrades warmly
And asked them each to tell her of their journey,
2390　And so they told her stories of strange sights,
And tales of terror caused by hungry trolls,
And storms at sea, and struggles on the land
With arrows shot by unseen enemies.
They hoped that she might have the time to hear
Their bard sing ballads, too, of Beowulf
If all their comrades could arrange to come,
But Hilda said it seemed unsuitable
To bring so broad a group above the harbor;
She said they climbed that cliff to be secluded
2400　And so the stairs they built would be too steep
And bothersome for any bearing burdens.
She said they would be glad to give the Geats
What help they could, and counsel on their course.
Yet, if they had an interest in such things,
She would be willing to provide them with

A bard whose ballads were most beautiful,
A swineherd who had somehow learned to sing
When angels touched him, tuned his troubled voice,
Commanding him to make engaging music
2410 To glorify the God who gave this gift.
Then Wiglaf would have been quite willing
Except that they were so consumed by travel
They needed now to rest and to renew
Their strength to sail and to pursue their quest.
Then Hilda had some counselors who were helpful
And gave the Geats advice on how to go.
They said the sea was safer than the land
Because of kings engaged in deadly conflict,
And so it seemed to them the Geats should sail,
2420 Providing victuals for a lengthy voyage;
Expecting they would spend some time at sea
They told them to allow a longish time
To reach a place not plagued by war and peril.
They spoke of certain spots along the coast
Where they might hope for haven in a harbor,
And reefs and rocks that had caused many wrecks.
The Geats were grateful for this useful guidance
And made their plans to move again next morning.

That night a gale began with gusts of wind
2430 That tore the trees, and soon a tempest raged.
The Geats made simple shelters with the sails
But those who once were washed with ocean waves
Were made yet damper by the driving downpour
That seemed to soak them deeper than the skin.
Next day, the downpour did not cease

And two whole days the tempest still continued
And then, too late to sail, the showers stopped
And Wiglaf sent some warriors to the woods
To forage in the forest for some food,

2440   To get some game and give them all fresh meat.
They came back rather quickly, having caught
Two deer, a buck and doe, and dragging with them
A fellow they had found who tried to flee,
Which made them think he threatened them.
They captured him and kept him to be questioned.
But Wiglaf thought he was not worth the worry;
He seemed to be a simple sort of man
Who had no weapons, was too weak to fight,
And held in both his hands a battered harp.

2450   With questioning, he said, "They call me Caedmon;
I have to herd the swine for Hilda's people.
But when they said that I must sing for strangers,
I feared, and so I fled into the forest."
"Are we so worrying to you?" Wiglaf asked.
"You came with clashing armor," Caedmon said,
"And warriors wielding spears and other weapons.
My harp, against such force, would hardly help;
But I have been uneasy anyway
About appearing in a public place.

2460   When, in the tavern, turns were being taken
And someone handed me the harp to hold
And lift my voice, I left and sat alone,
Afraid my friends would see me made a fool.
On one such winter night, I wept alone
To think I should be so ashamed to sing,

When, lo, an angel of the Lord came in
And touched my tongue and told me I should sing;
The vision vowed my voice would now be strong.
And suddenly I sang a new and wondrous psalm
2470   In praise of God, the Giver of all good.
And yet, each time, the terror still returns
And strangers strike great fear within my soul
Until I take the harp and touch the strings
And God unlocks my lips, and I am lost
In praise of God whose power placed me here."
"I wonder," Wiglaf said, "if you are willing
To sing your songs for some of us tonight.
Our hunters have brought home fresh game for us;
We can provide a visitor with venison."
2480   "I cannot stay," said Caedmon; "they require
To have my presence up at Hilda's house.
A poor man herding pigs must know his place
And come when called, and so I cannot stay.
Nor could I dine on deer; we do not eat
The flesh of beasts. Our food is always frugal;
We break our bread and drink our humble broth
And call it quite enough. I cannot stay;
I thank you though for thinking of me thus.
Your clan is kind; and yet, I cannot stay."
2490   "You cannot go," said Wiglaf; "captives can't
Just make their minds up that they wish to move.
I wish to warn you," Wiglaf said, "of this:
Our band of brothers brought you here to us,
And Hilda has already bade us hear you;
And so, at supper, we will hear you sing."

That night they feasted on the fresh-killed food
And beer the brothers brought to them from Hilda,
And Wiglaf called to Caedmon, "Come and sing,
Or else I too will touch your tongue."
2500   So Caedmon held his harp and hit the strings
And sang the song the Sovereign Lord had given
When first he found he need not fear to sing:
　　　"We give praise as we must * to the Master of heaven,
　　　The Creator's power * and purposes also,
　　　The Eternal One's work * and wonders as well,
　　　The Lord of Glory * beginner of all.
　　　First the Lord shaped * the shining sky-roof.
　　　The Holy One made it * for human beings."
The bard then said, "I sing a song like that:
2510   It is a ballad Beowulf brought back
From Hrothgar's hall when he had killed the monster.
With that he seized his harp and struck the strings:
　　　"I sing of human origins * in olden days
　　　When the All-Ruler * wrought the earth
　　　With glistening fields * girdled by water
　　　And set up in triumph * the sun and the moon
　　　As lights to illumine * the land and its dwellers
　　　And furnished all * the face of the earth
　　　With tree limbs and leaves. * The life was shaped
2520　　Of every creature * that creeps and moves."

"But can you sing us," Caedmon then inquired,
"A song of sojourn and of travelers' searching?"
"Of course I can," the bard responded quickly:
　　　"Weary and careworn * the wanderer travels,
　　　Homeless and helpless * hiding from fate,

Grieving at daybreak * when dawn arises,

Bringing the sunshine * and solace to others,

The death of his kin * and countless disasters.

Traveling the deep sea * swept by the breakers,

2530   Feeling the blast * of bitter north winds.

Day after day * the dreams of the heart

Send him on sea-streams * to shores far away,

Not knowing God's purpose * or plan for his fate.

All those know who bear it: * the bitter companionship,

Shoulder to shoulder, * sorrow provides

When friends forsake him * and his fortune is exile

Without any gifts * of gold to reward him

And earth's beauty dead. * He dreams then of hall feasts,

The sharing of treasure * and triumph with friends

2540   When his lord welcomed him * to wassail and joy;

Never again * will such gladness be his

Or the loving counsel * of his comrades and lord.

Here wealth is fleeting, * friends do not last,

Human life perishes, * passing soon away;

All of earth's fabric * fails at the end."

"Yes," Caedmon countered, "clearly you have known

A sadness and a sorrow in your searching;

But have you heard, in everything that happened,

Of One who wills the good of wanderers

2550   And guides them as they go toward their goal

Until the travelers find the end intended?

Let me sing of a wanderer * one who left everything

A man called Abraham * an alien and stranger

A herder of sheep * seeking a country

Who crossed mighty deserts * doing God's will;

Often he was hungry * homeless and weary
But angels attended him * at his tent's entrance.
He took bread and baked it * broke it for the strangers.
He offered them curds * and a calf he prepared.
2560 Then the Almighty * made him a promise:
You will have descendants * like the stars in number
And in your offspring * earth-folk will be blessed."

"Your harp-song helps me hold on to the hope
That God may give us guidance," Wiglaf said,
"The earth's wise Ruler always overcoming
The foes we find and filling us with strength."
"I promise I will pray that you may prosper,"
Said Caedmon. "With your kind concurrence now—
Delightful evening—I would like to leave
2570 And see that all my swine are in the sty.
I trust that Hilda has not ceased to hope
That she will see me safely back again."
"Then go," said Wiglaf. "Give our grateful thanks
To Hilda for your harp. You have been gracious;
And may the One you worship walk with us,
And guide the Geats, and govern us as well."

Next day the dawn was dark, but no rain fell;
The wind was with them as they went their way
And sailed a steady course toward the south.
2580 For two whole days they did not dare to stop
For fear of fighting forces on the shore.
The counselors had cautioned them with care
To seek for hidden sites and make them safe.
So when they came to coves that were secluded

They ranged a ring of guards around their camp
Lest trolls or troops of archers should attack
And find the Geatish forces undefended.
They were not told that trolls would trouble them
But thought it best that burning brands be ready
2590 Since no one knew what terrors stalked the night.
On certain days the morning sun would shine
And hearts were hopeful and the children happy,
But then a sudden shower would assail them
And drench their clothes and drive their spirits down.
A village on the shore was sometimes seen,
But Wiglaf was not willing to attack
As some insisted they should seek to do
To take the unprotected treasure there.
But Wiglaf wanted them to think of Wolferth,
2600 The sorrows he had suffered from the Swedes,
Who ambushed all his unsuspecting comrades
So almost none returned to tell the tale.
"We cannot count," he said, "from off the coast,
The warriors in the woods, or know what warning
Or message may have made its way to them.
We cannot be too careful, having come
This far, to fail or be defeated now."
So they continued to take care until
At last they saw such land as they had looked for
2610 And brought their boats to land and breathed a prayer
That here at last might be their hoped-for home.
The site they sought was not on open sea,
But flat and fertile land with spreading fields
And rivers running deep into the region,

A place where they could plow, and plant their crops,
And hope to build their homes, and reap a harvest,
With access open to the ocean's waves
For easy travel to take part in trade,
Which some would seek, while others sought a way
2620 To raid the rival clans around them;
But Wiglaf would not let them go to war.
For some it seemed a strange and alien life;
They longed to sail their ships up foreign streams
And then to fall in fierce and sudden fury
On victims: vandalize a peaceful village,
Or wreak their havoc on a humble home,
But, best of all, they thought, to battle bravely
With other men in armor like their own
And strike their spears against a linden shield
2630 And hear the hammering of swords on helmets
And deal the death-thrust in a fatal duel.
But Wiglaf would not let them go to war;
They questioned, carped, complained, and criticized
And yet, for many years, he would not yield.
The people prospered in a time of peace;
They worked to wall their homes with daub and wattle
And then laid thatch in thick layers on the roofs.
They tilled the level soil and sowed their seed
And gathered in the golden harvest grain
2640 Of wheat and oats and barley; others of them
Preferred to use their fields for flocks of sheep
And weave a warm, soft fabric with the wool.
As time went on a few men turned to trade
And sailed their ships in search of costly goods.

They took the finest fleeces they could find
And cloth the women wove from woolen thread
And carried cargo far across the sea
To come back bearing bowls of bronze
And cloaks and silver cups and combs
2650 And brooches, beads, and bottles made of glass,
And all the luxuries that ladies like.

The fields were fallow when they first arrived
But here and there they noticed humble huts
Of simple peasants scratching in the soil
And managing to make a meager living.
Some fled their fields in fear when ships arrived
But others would not leave the land they loved
And swore sincerely they would serve the Geats
And owe them honor, aiding them in conflict.
2660 In time, some smaller tribes came to them also
And so the Geats began to grow in numbers,
The realm they ruled became a wider region,
And comrades called on Wiglaf to be king
And be for them what Beowulf had been,
But Wiglaf would not wear a royal crown;
He said they should find someone else for that,
Until they told him all the tribe agreed.
Though people might oppose some policies,
They looked to him alone to be their leader.
2670 Reluctantly, at last he let them do
As they required and crown him as their king.
He said he would defend them from their foes
But would not go to war for gold or glory
Since these were frail rewards and faded fast

When put in place upon the funeral pyre.
Then Wiglaf warned them times would one day change
And kings would come who only cared for war;
These kings would take their treasure up in taxes
And make them give their sons to gain more glory
2680 And take their daughters to attend their wives.
But still they pressed him, so to please the people,
He let them call him king and make a crown
Though still he would not wear it willingly;
He seemed quite satisfied with simple things.
Then some of them began again to grumble;
They wished for one more warlike in his ways.
And yet, with times of peace, the people prospered;
Their fields were flourishing, their flocks increased,
And bigger, better homes were being built.
2690 It pleased the people that they could appear
To act like all the other tribes they knew
They built a handsome hall to hold their feasts
And celebrate their seasons of success,
A seemly hall where harp-songs would be heard
And bards could sing the ballads that brought back
The memory of many other moments,
Of former days and all the friends and foes
Who shaped the story that they so much loved.
They gathered gladly to rejoice again
2700 And fill their flagons up with foaming ale.

Then Yrfa, Wiglaf's wife, a gracious woman,
A kind and courteous queen, beloved by all,
And well attuned to tribal expectation,
Brought bowls of beer and carried them about,

To honor all who over many years,
Surviving various trials while on their voyage,
Had brought them here and helped create new homes;
And first she went to Wiglaf with a bowl,
In tribute to the leader of the tribe
2710 So he might drink a deep, thirst-quenching draft,
And then she favored Waelric, faithful friend,
And brought a bright and brimming cup of ale
To him who steadfast stood beside his lord,
And then to thanes who through their strength and wisdom
Had given useful guidance to the Geats.
The happy voices filled the hall; the harp
Resounded, skillful bards sang ancient sagas
And told new tales of how their tribe had traveled
Surmounting many perils undismayed.
2720 They linked their lines as they had learned to do,
Extolling with their wisely chosen words
The people who had proved their strength and prospered;
And so they celebrated their success.
They had not seen the hall that Hrothgar built
Nor did they give the gables golden trim
And yet they felt their feasting hall was finer
Than any on the island where they lived.
The fame of it spread far across the fens
Till Ranulf, ruler of the Saxon realm,
2730 Began to feel the Geats were gaining ground
That should be under Saxon sovereignty.
He called a counsel of his kingdom's leaders,
Those skilled in giving sound advice, and said,
"Another nation has annexed some land

That we consider to be Saxon soil.
We came here and we conquered British kings
And made them all submit to our command,
But now this foreign force is in our fields
And growing great and gaining strength each day,
2740 And soon we Saxons will become their slaves
Unless we can reclaim the land we conquered,
And slaughter and destroy unwelcome settlers.
Then his advisors vowed that these invaders
Must all be overcome and driven out.
So Ranulf rallied troops from all that region,
Instructing them to come with shields and spears,
To form a force of fearsome strength and size
To go against the unsuspecting Geats.
So, day by day, these troops were moving down
2750 Across the fens and coming ever closer.

The land between the two opposing tribes
Was flat and filled with slowly flowing streams
And so the Saxon forces moved by ship
Whenever rivers ran in their direction.
The marshes sometimes made such movement hard
And people had to pull their prows through swamp
And operate with ramps and ropes and rollers
To shift their ships to streams that served their purpose.
Yet, day by day, they kept on moving down
2760 Across the fens and coming ever closer.

In Ranulf's plan, his power would appear
So suddenly the Saxons' first assault
Would wipe away the Geatish warriors

Who would expect assault to come by sea
But would not look alertly to the land
Or station sentinels around a side
Where marshy places would impede the progress
Of troops intent on moving to attack.
The Saxon strategy made false assumptions
2770 Because the Geats encountered clans before
Who struck them suddenly from secret places,
The terrifying trolls and bowmen too,
And thus they always thought about such threats
And left some lookouts on the landward side
As well as sentinels to search the sea
For any evidence of enemies.
These watchers at a distance were aware
Of smoke ascending to the clouded sky
As if from far-off fires across the fens
2780 And noticed that each night the fires were nearer;
So then they went to Wiglaf with a warning
That troops of soldiers seemed to be assembling
And that the Geats should guard against attack.
Then Wiglaf made the men take certain measures:
To hone their swords and have their hauberks ready,
While Wiglaf, with some leading counselors, worked
To put in place a strong defensive plan
To stop the Saxons from destroying them.
Though now outnumbered, it was they who knew
2790 The fields they farmed, the rivers where they fished,
The length and breadth and limits of their land,

And could control the time when they attacked
And pick a place that would impede the foe.

The Saxons, struggling in the swampy ground,
Were wet and weary well before they reached
Their goal, the solid ground where stood the Geats,
But Saxon soldiers formed a seasoned army
Accustomed to the clash of arms in combat
And brutal battles with the British tribes.
2800 The dread of them endured in distant places
Wherever some had seen their savagery
Or heard what havoc Saxon hosts had wrought.
Nor did they doubt that they could do the same
To grind the Geatish folk into the ground;
They saw themselves as sovereigns of the land
And would not willingly provide a welcome
To strangers settling on the soil they claimed.
For two whole days the Geatish troops had toiled
To ready gear which years of rest had rusted;
2810 They sharpened spears and rubbed the grime from swords,
Repaired their shields, replacing worn-out parts,
The broken straps, and bosses that were bent,
And added other arrows to their quivers.
The two days full of tense activity
Had left them all on edge and out of sorts.
They often stopped and searched the sky for signals
And waited warily to hear a sentry's warning,
But silence seemed to reign; the only sound,
The heavy hammering of human hearts.
2820 But quiet often comes before a clash.

That evening, after all was set in order,
The Geats set guards in place and came together,
As Wiglaf wanted, when their work was done
To let the people all relax at last
With friends and foaming flagons, with no fear
Except the shadow of the strife to come.
The bards sang ballads of the bravery
Of heroes who had once defeated hordes
And boldly beaten back the strongest foes
2830   And crushed great kings and conquered provinces
And won renown, so now their names are known.
Then someone sang the saga of the journey
That brought them from afar to find this place.
He sang old songs long stored up in his mind
And made new words for many he remembered
Entwining them so he could tell new tales.
He wove together certain well-known words
With newer names they had not known before,
With tales of trolls and all the terror caused,
2840   And islanders who offered unused land,
And Hilda who had helped them on their way,
And those who died, who did not see their dream,
But who had fought to help them find these fields;
All these he sang in sweet and solemn tones
And let the last notes linger in the air.
The silence when he ceased his song was short.
The cups went round; the clamor quickly rose
As men concealed their mood with merriment
And fled their fear with cups of foaming ale.
2850   And somewhere near the Saxons also sang,

And drank their draughts of ale to stifle dread
And brashly boasted of their bravery,
Until a time of quiet came for all
And sleep descended and a silence fell
Across the fens, and then a cold wind came
And families felt it far away, and feared.

God's candle came up on a cloudless day
With sunlight shining on the sparkling grass.
The Geatish warriors grabbed their battle gear
2860 And soon assembled in a central place
And waited willingly for Wiglaf's coming.
A sentry stationed on a smallish hill,
Sharp-eyed, could see the enemy with ease,
And how the Saxon ships were sailing nearer
Along the languid streams that led them on,
But though he thought the threat was imminent
He took his time to tell them what he saw
Till he was certain they would soon succeed
In coming much too close to miss the quay
2870 From which the Geatish ships had sailed the seas.
So then he waved a warning down to Wiglaf,
Who made his way amid the waiting men.
"We do not deal with dragons here," said Wiglaf,
"But men no mightier than ourselves though more;
Yet each of us is able to defeat
A single Saxon, and a second one,
And then a third if that should be required.
When dauntless warriors do not fear to die,
If so they save their homes, their sons and daughters,
2880 And let them live forever in this land

That we have worked so long and hard to win.
Remember, dragons also die when doomed
By brave men willing to abate their breath.
So we will strike the Saxons such a blow
They'll rue the day they ran against our ranks
And Saxon blood will make the bards new ballads
As Geats unite to gain again the glory
That once was ours, and will be when we win."
Then men began to shout and strike their shields
But Wiglaf called for quiet, cautioned them
2890   That Saxons must not see them or suspect
That warriors were aware of them and ready
To strike as soon as they should step ashore.
Then Wiglaf ordered Wealric with the men
To hide themselves behind the little hill
That sloped down slowly to the marshy shore
While he himself put all his armor on.
He laced the leather greaves around his legs
And hauled the hot and heavy chain mail on,
2900   Its links forged long ago, a legacy
Of Eanmund, son and heir of Ohthere,
Whom Weohstan had slain in savage strife,
Unfortunate and friendless, far from home.
The helmet on his head was hardened iron
Embellished by a boar's head on the front;
He pushed his left hand through the leather loops
Behind the shining circle of his shield
And grasped his ancient sword, an heirloom also,
And took his stand where he could see the shore,
2910   Some halfway up the hill that hid his troops.

No sooner was he there than Saxon ships
Emerged, their masts above the marshy growth,
And soon their prows appeared, approaching shore.
Then Wiglaf slowly walked toward the ships
And said, "Be gone! This ground belongs to Geats;
We are a people proud to live in peace;
Who would not willingly engage in war,
But neither will we simply step aside
To let our land be seized unlawfully."

2920 But Ranulf, riding in the lead, arose
And said, "We do not come here seeking something
That is not ours to hold by ancient right.
We are prepared for peace if unopposed
And only ask that you give us your arms,
Your swords and shields and spears and other weapons,
And yield a yearly weight of yellow gold
Sufficient for the right to farm this land
As subjects should at all times to their sovereigns.
Bring arms and gold and we will gladly go."

2930 Deriding Ranulf, Wiglaf raised his voice
And said, "It seems to me your ears are stopped;
You have not heard the half of what I said.
I tell you, none should ever talk of tribute
Except for masters and their sullen slaves;
But for a people fearless, strong, and free,
Your speech is surely unacceptable.
So turn your ships and take your troops back home
Before they fall into the fens and drown,
For if they step ashore, you can be certain

2940 That many mourners will lament your death

And Saxon widows will be wailing long
At hearing how their noble heroes fell.
So tell your folk the tribute you can take:
The tribute of swift spears and sharp-edged swords
And grim engagement with the guardians
Who love this land and call on you to leave."
Replying, Ranulf pushed his prows until
They stuck in swampy water near the shore.
The warriors waded through the shallow water
2950 And gathered on the drier ground to glare
At Wiglaf, watching them not far away
And taunting them to come and take their tribute:
"My bright sword's poisoned point will pay you well
And slake its thirst by sipping Saxon blood."
But Ranulf had no need to haste or hurry;
He rearranged his ranks on rising ground
And shaped his soldiers in a solid shield-wall,
Each fighter fitted out in heavy fur
In keeping with the constant Saxon custom.
2960 Then, brandishing their burnished battle-axes
The Saxon shield-wall slowly moved uphill
As big drums boomed their baleful cadences.
Still Wiglaf walked ahead but turned to wait
At times and taunt the Saxon troops who trailed him
And call their vaunted courage into question,
Though they could hardly hear his hostile words
Above the booming of the battle drums.
As Wiglaf now approached the peak, he paused
And stretched the spear he carried toward the sky
2970 And waved it like a wand toward the Saxons

To signal those concealed beyond the summit
To fall upon the foe in all their fury.
The hidden ranks now rushed down with a roar
And smashed the shield-wall very near the center
To break the battle line, unbraced, in two
And send the remnant reeling in a rout,
Retreating to the ships, a tattered army,
Who found, aghast, a group of Geats behind them
Whom Waelric had brought with him from the woods.
2980   He circled with a small group to the side
In hope of hitting Ranulf from behind;
But Ranulf rallied men around his banner
And shaped their shields into a circle-wall
To face their furious foe on every side.
The Saxon slain lay scattered on the ground,
A few had even fled the battlefield
But Ranulf was not ready yet to rest
And Geats began to feel the greedy axes
That swung above the linden shields and struck
2990   Through helm and hauberk, splitting hapless heads
And sending sheets of blood down shields and swords;
The grass was grisly with the steaming gore.
The Saxons seemed secure within their circle;
The war-storm raged around their narrowed ranks
But now the Geats began to suffer grievously
And tire of taking the attack against
The fearful flailing of the fatal axes.
The bowmen did their best to shoot above
The Saxon shield wall with their stinging feathers
3000   And hit the gaps between the helm and hauberk

But all too few the foes who fell before them.
Then Wiglaf summoned to himself the strongest,
The best and bravest of his battered troops
And said, "The Saxon circle must be broken
Or else the outcome of this day will be
A Saxon victory, ourselves their slaves,
And all the trials and troubles of our trip
Be found a futile failure in the end.
So, all too often, other nations lost
3010   The freedom they had fought for when they failed
To stand with strength against usurping powers
And loved their lives above their liberty.
Let no one say we stepped back from the strife
For fear of falling in the battle-fury.
The goal of peace is more than gold or glory
And we must win our way to that reward
Through battle and, it may be, by our blood.
Let cowards quake, but let the brave men come!"

Then Wiglaf went again toward the wall
3020   Of shields and threw his spear with all his strength
And rushed at Ranulf, ramming shield on shield,
And striking sword against the swinging axe.
The clash and clamor of their combat rose
While all around them other rows were raging.
The battle-rush was bitter; brave men fell
In either army, old and young alike,
As soldiers strove to see who could be first
To deal out death to those whom fate had doomed,
For each side's aim was evil to the other.
3030   A Saxon soldier thrust his sword at Waelric,

Who countered with a crushing, crippling blow
That hit his helmet on the top so hard
He dropped to earth and Waelric dealt the death stroke.
A second Saxon warrior struck down Herbrund
But Waelric went to him and with his spear
He pierced the hapless man upon its point.
The spear went through his stomach, slaying him;
In clanging armor coat, he crashed to earth.
Then Waelric reached his hand to Herbrund, helping him
3040   To find his feet and join again the fray;
He slashed a Saxon buckler, splintered it,
And broke the arm that bore the battered shield.
A second swing cut through his sword arm also;
The warrior could no longer wield his weapons
Or grasp his gilded sword now on the ground.
A lethal stroke from Herbrund laid him low;
He sank down slowly on the bloody sod.
But meanwhile Wiglaf waged his war with Ranulf,
A deadly duel that others watched with dread,
3050   As, circling, each one sought a chance to strike
A fatal blow to finish off their feud.
Then Wiglaf slipped, the soil was soft with blood,
And Ranulf rushed in recklessly to kill;
But Wiglaf, leaning to his left, eluded
The eager axe and answered with a thrust,
A stab, that bit the Saxon in the side
And broke his charge and brought him briefly down.
He rose at once and ran in rage at Wiglaf;
His battle-blade came down with blinding speed
3060   And hit the helmet with such horrid force

That Wiglaf fell face-forward, floundering,
And would have died, but Waelric went to him
And stood above him struggling shield to shield
With Ranulf, blocked his blade and beat him back
Till Wiglaf once again regained his wits
And standing, swaying, raised his shaking sword
In time to take the Saxon's next attack.
But Ranulf, wounded as he was and weary,
Let slip his shield and Wiglaf's sword struck home.
3070 Then Ranulf fell, and all his fighters fled,
The Saxon losers, lacking loyalty,
Abandoned boats and fled the battlefield
To leave their leader lying on the earth
And flee on foot across the spreading fens,
And so were swallowed by the swampy ground.

But then they found that in the final fray
An arrow aimed at someone else
Had missed its mark and somehow made its way
By chance to hit a chink in Wiglaf's chain mail
3080 And hit him near the heart, a heinous blow
That doomed him, though he did not die until
He first had finished Ranulf's fighting days,
Then walked toward a wall where he could sit
And speak to those who stood around in sorrow
To see the lord who led them lying there,
The gallant Geatish leader on the ground.
Then Waelric brought him water, wet his brow,
And held his head to help him as he spoke:
"We ventured on our voyage with a vision
3090 And sought a place of peace where we might prosper;

The Saxons may not soon resume the struggle,
Returning once again to test our temper,
But rivalries will rise within our ranks
And some will seek to steal the wealth of others,
For now I know it is not in our nature
To help and heal and never turn to harm,
For envy is our inner enemy
And greed for gain and glory guides too many.
I said I could not conquer all who came
3100   Against the Geats and guard you by myself
Nor be for you what Beowulf had been,
Who slew the monsters by his single strength,
But that may be our benefit, not bane.
When work is shared, society is stronger;
Our world is weak when all depend on one,
So seek for ways to share in leadership
And learn a larger loyalty that flows
From each to all, from all to everyone;
And dare a greater dream, still dim
3110   But not beyond the yearning of the years,
That all of us who live here on this island
May find a path to peace so all may prosper
And flourish free of fears of worldly foes.
I call to mind the country Caedmon sang,
Where all our human hearts at last are healed
And senseless striving is forever stilled.
My journey is not over; I go on
In hope to reach the Heaven-Ruler's realm.
I want my body buried by my friends,
3120   Not placed upon a pyre like Beowulf's

Nor sent off on the sea like that of Scyld,
But dig my grave in ground that we have gained
By valiant voyaging and victory,
And make a mound there to remember me,
And so that some will ask to hear the story,
The ancient story of our origins,
And how we came in quest of quiet peace
And slew the Saxon foe to save our freedom."

The grieving Geats began to carry out
3130   The wish expressed in Wiglaf's final words.
They sought a ship that would be suitable
And picked their proudest boat; its ring-necked prow
Had brought them safely through the storm and stress
Of ocean waves and weeks of wandering
And left them all at last in this good land.
So would the warrior and water-rider
Who crossed the seas and conquered ocean currents,
The wanderers who faced the world's strong waves,
Now sail again to seek a farther shore
3140   Unwashed by waves, unwearied by earth's tumult.

They brought the boat about, bow end away;
Then, waiting till the tide had almost turned
To have the hull as high as possible,
They pulled the prow to place it in position
On rollers they arranged along the route
Between the tide and place they had determined
To be the best to use for burial.
With ropes they rolled it up the riverbank
To move along a fairly level lane,

3150   Then up a steeper slope—the men now sweating—
To find the chosen pasture, flat and fair,
In which a crew had carved a cavity
With space enough to hold the splendid ship.
They rolled it up a ramp to reach this pit
And bring the boat above the burial place.
They weighted one end down and took away
The rollers that were at the other end
So they could tilt the ship into the tomb;
Then mauls removed the rollers that remained

3160   To let the ship subside into the space.
They braced the bottom then by bringing earth
And settling shovelfuls around the sides.
Inside the boat they built a sort of box
By putting planks in place and nailing them,
To make a room, a royal resting place.
Some sturdy pegs were set along one side
To hold a cast-iron cauldron and some cups;
A royal scepter, shield, and sharpened spears
Were wedged in place against the western wall.

3170   Within the center of the space they set
The coffin, carried carefully the corpse
And lowered it with loyal and loving arms.
They fitted at his feet some folded cloth,
A hammer, drinking horn, and hanging bowls,
A pillow, gaming pieces, pair of shoes,
Some combs, a cap of fur, a coil of tape,
Three burrwood bottles, buckles large and small,
A ladle, lances, and a leather bag;
They covered this collection with a cloak

3180   Of woven wool that he had often worn.
   They hammered home the top with heavy blows
   Then laid a lyre upon the coffin lid
   And cast another cloak across the coffin;
   On that they set a shining silver dish
   Embossed with beasts and bordered with a braid.
   They offered all these objects to provide
   A truly worthy tribute to their leader,
   The honor that was owed by all of them,
   And also all that Wiglaf would be wanting
3190   To fight and feast in unknown future years.
   At last they placed a lamp and lighted it
   And closed the cover of the room they crafted.

   Then there was wailing of the women in their woe
   Who feared that foes would fall upon them
   If Wiglaf was not with them as their leader,
   While warriors stood about in solemn silence
   And watched the coffin, wondering how well
   Another leader would allot their lives,
   For Wiglaf always wanted one thing only:
3200   A place where all could put down roots and prosper.
   No trolls or troubles turned him from that goal;
   He brought them through and beat their foes in battle,
   But now they knew another leader must
   Be chosen as their chief, to challenge them.
   Would he seek wars to wage, would he be weak,
   Would he make plans for peace so they might prosper?
   So much would be demanded of this man
   Whom they would seek to serve with all their strength,
   And so they faced the future, and they feared.

3210 Then Waelric said, "I wish that Wiglaf would
       Bequeath his questing courage to us all
       But we must seek his spirit in ourselves
       To face our people's future unafraid,
       And hope that he who brought us safely here
       Has left a legacy of loyalty
       To give the Geats the gift of unity.
       We have no Beowulf to bear our burdens
       So each of us must offer what we can;
       So may we move ahead, and yet remember."

3220 Then all the earth which had been taken out,
       The sod and soil, was shoveled slowly in,
       And other earth was added to the pile
       To make the mound that Wiglaf had demanded,
       A hillock high above the heaving sea,
       That would be seen by sailors in their ships
       Arriving with new riches on the river;
       The mast remained protruding from the mound
       And held up high toward the heavens
       A banner with a bear embroidered on it
3230 Until with passing time the timber rotted,
       Fell down, and disappeared, and memory dimmed,
       And no one still remained who knew the name,
       What body had been buried in the barrow,
       Or how he died or deeds that he had done.

Notes on the Text

Line

1 "Hwaet!" The first word of *Beowulf* is variously translated "What!," "Lo!," "Indeed," "Attend." Although it is the ancestor of the English word "what," its purpose here in a formulaic opening is to call for attention and we have therefore begun with that word.

1–18 The final passage of *Beowulf* describes the funeral pyre on which he was cremated amid expressions of fear for the future.

28–31 Beowulf had met his death in combat with a dragon which had been ravaging the countryside in vengeance for the theft of a cup from his treasure trove.

35 *Beowulf* begins with the tale of how King Hrothgar built a great mead-hall named Heorot to celebrate his victories.

47–52 Wiglaf had come to the aid of Beowulf in his final combat with the dragon. He is described as the "son of Weohstan" and Beowulf speaks of him as the "last man of our tribe, the race of Waegmundings." He is, then, the logical successor to Beowulf. He and Beowulf are the only named characters from *Beowulf* who appear in *Beyond Beowulf*.

65 Grendel is the name of the monster slain by Beowulf early in his career.

80–84 These fears and forebodings are discussed at the end of *Beowulf*.

197–214 The reference here is to a speech in lines 2900–3028 of *Beowulf* and, specifically, lines 2922 and 3001 that speak of a threat from the Swedes. The Geats, the tribe of Beowulf and Wiglaf, lived in Sweden, perhaps in the area now known as Götland, an south of the area inhabited then by the Swedes.

233 Hygelac (also given as Higlac and Higelac in translations) was king of the Geats at the outset of Beowulf and is Beowulf's uncle. He is the one character in Beowulf whose existence is confirmed by other sources. He was killed during a raid on the Franks about the year 521 a.d. This would place Beowulf's death toward the end of that century and somewhat early for the events described in *Beyond Beowulf*. Beowulf reported back to Hygelac after his victory over Grendel and Grendel's mother.

234ff. Hygelac's death, in the battle at Ravenswood (Hrefnes-holt), is described by the Messenger in lines 2419–2496.

242ff. This tale of Beowulf is not to be found in the original and seems to draw on later tales of Eric the Red and Leif Eriksson—but perhaps they were moved to sail west by tales of Beowulf's voyage.

361–362 A bard sings of the creation of the earth in *Beowulf*, lines 91–99.

405ff. The fight mentioned here is described in more detail in *Beowulf*, lines 2354ff. and lines 2500ff. Beowulf is said to have swum back to Sweden from Frisia carrying the armor of thirty warriors in his arms.

457ff. See lines 2920ff. of *Beowulf*

471 The Scylfings are Swedes; not to be confused with the Scyldings (see line 763 below), who are Danes.

497ff. The description of this battle and other later battles draws on the Old English poem *The Battle of Malden* as well as battles scenes in Beowulf.

519 "He had no breath to boast of battle-deeds." A common device in the Old English poetic style, a feature of Beowulf in particular, is *litotes*, a deliberately strong understatement, often negative in form.

568 A subject much discussed by *Beowulf* scholars is the knowledge the significance of the references to the Bible in *Beowulf*. While the *Beowulf* poet probably inhabited a Christian world himself, he seems careful not to imply a similar level of knowledge for those of whom he writes—but he does make reference from time to time to the limits of their knowledge.

660ff. This incident is referred to first in lines 2596–2599 of *Beowulf* and again in lines 2864–2891. It is one of many places in which the importance of loyalty is emphasized.

720–721 The building of Beowulf's barrow is recorded in lines 3156–3159 of *Beowulf*.

756–762 Hrothgar's pledge is reported in lines 1854–1865 of *Beowulf*.

771 The Scyldings, descendants of Scyld (also spelled Scild in some translations), are the Danes. Hrothgar is Scyld's great-grandson.

792–810 Here I have tried to reflect the language of two Old English poems known as *The Wanderer* and *The Seafarer*.

872ff. This episode is modeled on the story of Beowulf's arrival in Denmark (*Beowulf,* lines 229ff): he was greeted by a wary coastguard, sent up to Hrothgar's hall, greeted again by a guard, and finally admitted to the king's presence.

932–935 The burning of Heorot is foreshadowed in lines 82–85 of *Beowulf,* immediately after the report of its building.

1040–1046 In *Beowulf,* lines 815–824, we hear how Beowulf tore off Grendel's arm and in lines 834–836 how he nailed it to the gable of Heorot.

1266ff. There are various traditions concerning trolls. Some say that they turn to stone if exposed to sunlight; others that they melt when exposed to fire. I have followed the latter tradition.

1537–1543 This is my translation of Hrothgar's speech in lines 1763–1768 of *Beowulf*

1732–1740 This history is given in the opening lines of *Beowulf,* lines 4–79.

1833ff. The following episode is set in the Orkney Islands, north of the Scottish mainland.

1910–1913 The reference here is to the Stones of Stenness and Maes Howe, also in Orkney.

1941–1956 The guide books say that Vikings broke into Maes Howe about the year 1000 and scrawled runes on the walls in frustration when they failed to find treasure—but perhaps the Geats had broken into it earlier and reacted in the same way.

1962 The "hollow hills" of the draugrs are a part of Orkney folklore.

2214–2330 The community at Lindisfarne was founded by St. Aidan, who arrived from Iona in 635 a.d.

2360ff. The Abbess Hilda founded the community at Whitby in 657 a.d. It included both men and women under her rule.

2450ff. Caedmon was a member of Hilda's community. The story he tells here of how he became a poet is all that is known of him.

2503–2508 This is my translation of Caedmon's hymn to the Creator, the earliest English poem. Here, as with the subsequent bardic songs, I have conformed much more closely to the pattern of Old English poetry. Each line has four stresses and there is a caesura between the two half lines. The first stressed syllable of the second half line provides the alliterated letter which is then matched by one or two of the stressed syllables in the first half line.

2513–2520 This is my translation of a passage in *Beowulf* (lines 91–98). The similarity between this passage and Caedmon's hymn is striking.

2524–2545 This poem is my composition but based on an Early English poem called *The Wanderer.*

2610ff. Sutton Hoo is an historic site in East Anglia, thought to have been settled in the early 7th century. There are reasons to believe that the settlers who created the burial mounds there had come from Sweden, perhaps from Götland. The best discussion of this subject is to be found in *The Origins of Beowulf and the Pre-Viking Kingdom of East Anglia* by Sam Newton (cf. Bibliography.)

2648ff. The items mentioned here have been found at Sutton Hoo.

2676–2680 There is a deliberate echo here in Wiglaf's warning about future kings of the warning Samuel gave the people of Israel (I Samuel 810–18).

2729 Ranulf is my own creation, but there were Saxon kings of East Anglia in the early seventh century with similar names.

2859ff There are several battle descriptions in *Beowulf*; the story of *The Fight at Finnsburh*, (lines 1068–1159) is one example. The Early English poem *The Battle of Malden* is also helpful. The Bernard Cornwell novels about the Arthurian legend provides some very careful description of Saxon and British armor and battles.

3076ff. Wiglaf's death scene is similar in many ways to Beowulf's death scene (*Beowulf*, lines 2715–2722).

3129ff. The details of the ship burial are based on the descriptions given in *Sutton Hoo, Burial Mound of Kings* by Martin Carver (cf. Bibliography.)

Annotated Bibliography

Translations of *Beowulf*:

Chickering, Howell D., Jr. *Beowulf, a Dual Language Edition*. New York: Anchor Books, Doubleday, 1977. This is the fullest edition I know of, complete with the Early English text and extensive notes and commentary. The translation makes no effort to preserve the alliteration.

Heaney, Seamus. *Beowulf, a New Verse Translation*. New York: Farrar, Straus and Giroux, 2000. Includes the Early English text.

Jack, George. *Beowulf, A Student Edition*. Oxford: Oxford University Press, 1994. The original text with introduction, running glossary, and supplemental glossary; no translation.

Porter, John. *Beowulf, Text and Translation*. Middlesex, England: Anglo-Saxon Books, 1991. A useful, nearly literal translation with the Early English text.

Raffel, Burton. *Beowulf*. New York: Penguin Books, Ltd., 1963. A verse translation that deals freely with the alliteration but does not keep to the divided line of the Early English or provide the original text.

Rebsamen, Frederick. *Beowulf, a Verse Translation*. New York: Icon Editions, 1991. A very good translation that preserves the pattern of the Early English poetry.

Editions of Early English Poetry:

Hamer, Richard. *A Choice of Anglo-Saxon Verse, Selected with an Introduction and a Parallel Verse Translation.* London: Faber and Faber, 1970. No particular effort has been made to preserve the alliteration; original text is provided.

Kennedy, Charles W. *An Anthology of Old English Poetry.* New York: Oxford University Press, 1960. An alliterative translation without the original text.

Discussions of the relationship between *Beowulf* and Sutton Hoo and East Anglia:

Carver, Martin. *Sutton Hoo, Burial Ground of Kings?* London: British Museum Press, 1998. A careful study of the burial mounds at Sutton Hoo and the possible significance of the findings.

Newton, Sam. *The Origins of Beowulf and the Pre-Viking Kingdom of East Anglia.* Cambridge, England: D.S. Brewer, 1994. An analysis of the relationships between Beowulf and East Anglia centered on texts and genealogies.

Box 1724
Sharon, CT 06069

clw56@MigrashSharon.com
860-364-1139

978-0-595-67489-3
0-595-67489-5